The GUNSLINGER

Also by Lorraine Heath

The
GUNSLINGER

LORRAINE
HEATH

**(A version of this work originally appeared in the
print anthology *To Tame a Texan*, under the title
"Long Stretch of Lonesome")**

AVONIMPULSE
An Imprint of HarperCollinsPublishers

Excerpt from *Once More, My Darling Rogue* copyright © 2014 by Jan Nowasky.

EPub Edition JULY 2014 ISBN: 9780062353078

Print Edition ISBN: 9780062353108

10 9 8 7 6 5 4 3 2

In loving memory of Pete Denby, who cast a tall shadow.

Chapter 1

Lonesome, Texas
1884

CHANCE WILDER WAS a man with his back against the wall.

Finding comfort in the rough wood of the saloon pressing against his slender shoulders, his chair tilted back, he studied the comin's and goin's, constantly alert to the potential for trouble. He didn't fear the bullet that might hit him dead on. It was the one that would sneak up from behind that weighed heavily on his mind.

He scrutinized the young fella—standing with his elbow perched on the bar—who hadn't taken his eyes off Chance since Chance sauntered through the saloon doors. He'd watched the man down half a bottle of whiskey, his fingers caressing the butt of his gun in between swallows as though unable to find courage in either the liquor or the sidearm. He figured the fidgeting gent would meet his Maker before Chance rode out of town.

With a slight shift in his hips, Chance eased forward and the chair's front legs hit the wooden floor with a resounding thud. The saloon suddenly became more hushed than a prayer meeting as wary eyes homed in on him. He could sense the anticipation on the air, the thrumming of excitement that made every last one of them hypocritical vultures.

His gaze cautiously roaming the room, he slowly tipped the bottle of whiskey until he'd refilled his glass without so much as a splash, his hand steady as a rock. In his line of work, he relied on a steadfast hand. He set down the bottle, picked up the glass, and dropped back against the wall, balancing the chair with the confident ease that he used when cradling his gun in the palm of his left hand.

He sipped on the amber liquid like a man in no hurry—which he was. He had no one waiting on him, hadn't had anyone waiting on him since he'd killed his first man at fourteen.

He heard one cowboy clear his throat and the harsh whisper of another. He didn't have to hear the words to know what they were discussing.

Every person in the saloon—every citizen in the town—wanted to know who Chance Wilder had come to Lonesome, Texas, to kill.

TOBY MADISON HURTLED himself through the swinging doors of the saloon. The thick cigar and cigarette smoke burned his eyes, while the stench of sour whiskey and sweating bodies made him want to puke. Or maybe it was the thick blood trickling down the back of his throat that caused his stomach to lurch. He thought the bully might have busted his nose.

"Hey, boy, get out," a giant cowboy ordered, clamping a large hand onto Toby's shoulder.

Toby jerked free, his frenzied gaze darting over the glaring faces. He hadn't expected half the men in town to lollygag in the saloon this time of day. He'd never find the one for whom he was desperately searching.

Then he realized that everyone was crowded to the right of the bar, leaving open space that he could see out of the corner of his eye. He swung around. His gut knotted up tighter than a hangman's noose when he saw the stranger in the black duster sitting in the far corner, alone, his chair tipped back and his silver eyes narrowed as thinly as the sharp-edged blade of a Bowie knife.

Toby swallowed hard and limped hurriedly across the room. "You the gun-for-hire everybody's talkin' about? Are you Chance Wilder?"

The man's eyes narrowed further, and Toby figured he could slice a fella open just by looking at him. "If'n you are, I wanna hire you."

"Already been hired," Wilder replied in a quiet raspy voice that still managed to echo around the saloon and cause a shiver to crawl down Toby's spine.

He heard gasps and feverish whispers. Even with the blood trailing down his throat, his mouth went dry. "But them bullies is beating up my sister. I want you to make 'em leave her be."

"You look old enough to do the job."

"I tried to stop 'em from hurtin' Lil, but there's five of 'em—"

The bartender grabbed him, his beefy fingers biting into Toby's skinny arm. Toby bucked with all his might but couldn't wrestle free of the relentless grip. Panic clawed through him. He had to save Lil.

"This is no place for you, boy," his captor barked as he hauled Toby across the room like the sack of flour he'd dropped when the bullies grabbed his sister and dragged her behind the general store.

Desperation edged Toby's words as he fought frantically to keep his eyes on Wilder. "I'll pay you everything, everything I got!"

Wilder slammed the front legs of his chair against the floor. The bartender froze. Toby wrenched away and moved beyond reach. The gunslinger unfolded his tall, lean body and tugged on the brim of his black Stetson.

"What the hell," he murmured. "I ain't never been paid everything before."

"You want to steer clear of this mess," the bartender said in a voice that Toby didn't think sounded too sure of what it was saying.

Wilder pulled one side of his black duster back to reveal a pearl-handled gun housed in a holster slung low on his hip. *Everything* is a hell of a lot, mister. You gonna better the kid's offer?"

"No . . . no, sir," the bartender stammered.

"Then don't tell me my business, because you ain't paid for the privilege."

"We gotta hurry," Toby announced as he scurried out of the saloon. He heard Wilder's spurs jangling as he followed. He figured Lil was gonna have a cow when she found out he had hired a gun to save her. But he didn't see as he'd had a choice.

CHANCE SAUNTERED AFTER the towheaded kid, lengthening his stride as they distanced themselves from the saloon. Skinny as a willow branch, the boy couldn't be any older than seven or eight. But he had spunk. Chance had to give him that. And if he wasn't mistaken, the boy had a broken nose. He hadn't noticed it until the bartender grabbed the kid to haul him out. It had to hurt like hell, but the boy's only worry seemed to be his sister. Chance chuckled low. He was looking forward to receiving everything—and how much trouble could it be to chase a few bullies away from a little girl?

With his booted feet pounding the boardwalk, the boy raced past the general store, flew around a corner, and disappeared between two buildings. Stepping over the split sack of flour that dusted the wooden slats, Chance gave the wagon in front of the general store a passing glance. Then he heard the kid's indignant yell, quickened his pace, charged into the alleyway, and staggered to a halt as five men gave him an insolent glance, before returning to their business.

A cowboy in a battered brown hat had one arm wrapped around the boy and was pressing the business end of a pistol to his temple. The boy stood as still as a stone statue, his eyes trained on his sister—pinned against the wall by a man large enough to crush her. Her skirt and petticoats were hiked up to her thighs . . . up to her slender womanly thighs, revealing slender ankles and longs legs that might stretch clear up to her throat. Her burnished hair in wild disarray tumbled past her shoulders. With each labored breath she took, her torn bodice revealed the creamy curve of a small breast. Scratches marred alabaster skin that had probably never seen the sun before that moment. Blood trailed down from a split lower lip and a bruise was forming high on her cheek.

Her captor shifted, pressed a beefy forearm against her delicate throat and began to unfasten his britches with his other hand. "Figured you'd stop fighting with the right incentive," he drawled.

Defiance shot into her startling cornflower blue eyes and quickly faded into acceptance of her fate. She must have fought like a wildcat to hold the brutish men at bay as long as she had.

"Don't believe the lady has much interest in your style," Chance said with feigned calmness, wondering why no one had come to her defense until now.

The apparent leader snapped his head around and snarled, "This ain't none of your concern."

Chance slipped a matchstick out of his shirt pocket and wedged it between his teeth. In his youth he'd discovered that he had the embarrassing habit of rolling out his tongue when he slid the gun from his holster. As if looking like a panting dog in the middle of a gunfight wasn't bad enough, he'd damn near bit off his tongue a time or two. Gnawing on the matchstick kept his tongue behind his teeth where it belonged. And it had the added advantage of making him look a little more dangerous. "The boy paid me to make it my concern."

"Toby," the woman gasped low, shaking her head at her brother. Chance's gut clenched. Her raspy voice sounded like she'd just crawled out of bed after a long night's sleep or an even longer night of lovemakin'.

"He's gonna save you!" the boy assured her, proudly puffing out his chest even though he still had the barrel of a six-shooter kissing his temple. Chase tried to remember what the boy had called his sister—Lydia? Lilly? Lil? That was it. Lil.

The leader released a sharp bark of laughter. "Head out, mister."

"Where I come from, men don't paw ladies who don't want to be pawed," Chase told him.

"Well, she ain't no lady. She's a whore. Jack Ward's whore."

She let loose a stream of spittle that hit her insulter in the eye. He swung his arm back—

"Don't even think it," Chance commanded in a tone rife with authority. "Can't tolerate a man who hits a woman."

The brute lifted a corner of his mouth in a sneer. "That so?"

"Yep, that's so." He wrapped his fingers around the edge of his duster and drew it aside, hooking it behind his gun.

One of the other men started to twitch, his beady little eyes growing round. "Hey, Wade, I'm thinking this might be that fella—"

"Shut up," Wade growled, knocking the woman to the ground before planting his feet apart, facing Chance squarely and issuing his challenge. "Stop me from hitting her."

Chance met and held each man's gaze briefly before letting his icy glare settle on the one itching for a fight. "I don't want any misunderstandings here. I need your boys to know that I'll kill every man who draws a gun."

"Holy hell," the nervous man said, throwing up his arms. "He's the gunslinger, Wade. I ain't gettin' myself killed over no woman."

Wade's hideous smile faltered. "That so? You the gunslinger?"

"He sure is!" Toby yelled. "And he's fast, too. Faster than anybody!"

"They say you're reckless and wilder than most," Wade said, doubt laced through his voice. "They say you've killed twenty-four men."

Chance gave a short nod. "That's what they say." He slid his gaze over to the man who still held the boy. "The first bullet goes right between your eyes if your gun ain't holstered by the time mine clears leather."

With a shaking hand, the man slid his gun into his holster and released the boy. "This ain't my fight."

Chance jerked his head to the side. "Get outta here, boy."

The youngster rushed to where his sister was crouched against the wall. He curled up in her lap and she wrapped her arms closely around him. That wasn't exactly what Chance had in mind for the kid. He didn't like for children to see death. At its best, it was an ugly sight. At its worst, it guaranteed nightmares.

He locked his focus squarely onto Wade. "If you and your friends want to just stroll on outta here—"

Wade went for his gun. Everything else seemed to unfold within the same excruciatingly slow moment. Chance slid his gun from his holster, heard an explosion, and felt a bullet bite into his shoulder as he hit the dirt, rolled, aimed, and fired. Surprise flittered across Wade's face—just before he crumpled into a lifeless heap.

Chance struggled to his feet. The woman stared at him in horror, as though she'd forgotten the man he just killed had planned to brutally abuse her. He'd long ago accepted that the reality of death usually made people forget that only moments before they'd desperately prayed that the deceased would die. "That your wagon in front of the general store?" he asked.

She gave a brusque nod. Chance pinned three of the men with a steely-eyed glare. "Reckon she'd appreciate it if you'd finish loading it for her." They bobbed their heads like apples tossed into a barrel of water. "See that you get her a new sack of flour while you're at it."

They scurried off to do his bidding. He looked at the man who'd held the boy earlier. As much as he wanted to shoot him in the foot for terrorizing a child, he merely said, "Fetch the sheriff."

The man balked. "Wade drew first."

Chance nodded slowly. "Yep. Be sure you tell him that 'cuz I can't tolerate liars and you just saw what happens to people who do things I can't tolerate."

The man was still nodding when he disappeared around the corner.

The boy scrambled out of his sister's lap and came to stand before Chance, his head bent back as he looked up at him with something akin to hero worship reflected in his eyes. "You saved Lil." The boy dug a hand into the pocket of his britches. "I'm gonna pay you everything just like I promised."

Chance held out his hand, and the boy dumped "everything" into his cupped palm: a length of frayed string, a rusty harmonica, and a bent penny.

Chapter 2

LILLIAN MADISON STARED straight ahead as she guided the wagon home. She found it impossible to believe that her brother had hired a man to protect her—or that the man seemed intent on honoring his end of the bargain until she was safe behind locked doors.

She cast a sideways glance at Chance Wilder. Sitting rigidly on a dun-colored horse, he rode beside the wagon, his face set in tight, unforgiving lines. She'd heard of him, of course. They sung ballads about him and penned dime novels based on his exploits. He had a reputation for drifting into a town and not leaving until he killed someone. She supposed now that Wade would be making use of a plot in the church cemetery, Wilder would move on in search of more excitement. She'd be glad to be rid of him. How could a man kill with no remorse? His eyes had been icy, calculating. He had moved with the grace of a striking snake when he jerked his gun from his holster, holding the weapon as though it was a part of him. She shuddered with the memories of his swift, smooth motions that had resulted in a man dying.

"Have you really killed twenty-four men?" Toby asked, bouncing energetically on the wagon seat, turning toward Wilder. She had taken her brother to see the doctor before they left town. The physician stuffed cotton up Toby's nostrils to halt the bleeding from his broken nose. He had to breathe through his mouth, and when he talked, his voice honked like a goose. She imagined the squawking could easily grate on the nerves of a man like Wilder.

"That's what they say," Wilder replied in a flat voice.

"Reckon it's twenty-five now on account of Wade dying."

"Reckon so."

"How do you keep count?" Toby asked. "Do you notch your gun belt?"

Wilder remained silent.

"I heard gunslingers notch their gun belt. Want me to do it for you—notch your gun belt, I mean?"

"Nope."

"But how will you remember?"

"Boy, I do my damnedest to forget."

"Then how do you keep count?"

Wilder ignored the question. Lillian wanted to explain to him that she couldn't abide anyone ignoring a child, no matter how bothersome he became. But she had no desire to engage him in conversation. He may have saved her from a horrible fate, but he left death in his wake, and seemed not to be the least bit bothered by it. He was a cold, hard man. Toby had given the man his dearest possessions, and Wilder had dropped the treasured gifts into his duster pocket as though they were less valuable than dirt.

"You ever been to Houston?" Toby asked. "Me and Lil used to live in Houston."

Silence.

"What about Austin? You ever been there? Me and Lil got to spend the night in a hotel there when we was moving here. It's only a day's ride away. I bet you come through there on your way here."

Silence stretched between the man and the boy. Toby rolled his tiny shoulders forward, and Lillian knew Wilder's disinterest had hurt her brother's feelings. She wanted to slap the man. She'd spare Toby from all the hurt in the world if she could. It was the reason she had accepted the land and the house that Jack Ward offered her.

If only she'd realized all the trouble that bit of foolishness would cause.

Toby gave her a lopsided grin that revealed his latest missing tooth. "Don't think he likes to talk."

"Seems not." She slipped her arm around him and drew him up against her side, hugging him fiercely. "But you need to know: he didn't save me. You did."

The only one in this world who loved her, never judged her.

She drew the horses to a halt in front of the white clapboard house. After climbing down from the wagon, she trudged over to Wilder. She peered up at his cold, implacable face. "We're home now—safe. I'd appreciate it if you'd head back to town."

Only his silver eyes moved as he slid his gaze to her. "The boy paid me . . . *everything*. Never had *everything* before . . ."

Slowly he lowered his eyelids, slumped forward and tumbled off his horse. With a small startled screech, Lillian jumped back as he landed with a thud near her feet.

"Gawd Almighty!" Toby cried, scrambling down from the wagon and skidding to his knees beside Wilder, whose duster had parted to reveal a white shirt soaked in bright crimson blood. Lillian thought she might be ill.

Toby snapped his head around, fear reflected in his blue eyes. "He got shot. Why didn't he say something when we was at the doctor's?"

Shaking her head, she knelt beside Wilder and gingerly unbuttoned his shirt. Carefully lifting the material and peering beneath it, she saw the ragged, gaping hole still oozing blood from his shoulder.

"He's bleedin' something awful," Toby said. "You gotta help him, Lil."

Lillian hesitated. If she helped a man who made a living killing others, would she, in effect, become an accomplice to future killings? If she left him as he was, perhaps he would not survive, and no one else would die. But could her conscience live with that? Let one man die to save others, allow others to be killed to save one man? What was her debt to him?

He had come to Lonesome for a reason—to kill someone. As much as she hoped Wade had been his intended prey, she thought it highly unlikely. So someone else's name was etched on one of his bullets.

Toby slipped his small hands beneath the man's shoulders and struggled to lift him. "Come on, Lil. We gotta get him into the house." He raised his troubled gaze to hers. "He saved you!"

She considered what Wade might have done to her if this gunslinger hadn't shown up. No one would have stopped him. Everyone in town believed she deserved that sort of treatment.

Toby strained to heft the man. Wilder's hat tumbled off his head to reveal a riot of ash blond curls. His hair looked incredibly soft, like Toby's had as a baby. She hadn't expected that of a man who killed others to make money. Unconscious, his face completely relaxed, he looked young, much younger than she'd originally thought he was.

"Help me, Lil," Toby pleaded with labored breaths.

How could she explain her dilemma to her innocent brother? What sort of example would she be setting if she left him to die? She couldn't control this man's actions. She could only control her own. Giving Toby a sharp nod, she bent to help her brother carry the hired gun into the house.

THE RAGING FIRE burned through his shoulder. Chance wanted to stay huddled behind the wall of agony, but the softness beckoned him, touched him, spoke to him.

He struggled to open his eyes. He was in a room he

didn't recognize, beneath a quilt that didn't belong to him. His right shoulder was swathed in bandages. The woman sat on the edge of the bed, patting a warm damp cloth over his bare chest, humming a tune—"Red River Valley." Ruby shadows shimmered over her hair. He decided the muted shades were caused by the flame from the lamp sitting on the bedside table. She appeared young and innocent, too innocent to be an old man's whore. He knew all about Jack Ward because the man's family had paid him to come to Lonesome.

"What's Lil short for?" he croaked.

Her hand stilled, right above his pounding heart. "Lillian. Lillian Madison."

"Pretty name." A tinge of scarlet crept into her cheeks, and he knew he could easily drown within the fiery blue depths of her eyes if he wasn't careful. Fortunately, experience had tempered him into cautiousness.

"You should have told someone you'd been shot," she scolded, as though he were a child to be looked after.

"Would have brought out the vultures," he said wearily.

Her delicate brows knit together. "The vultures?"

"Men looking to gain a quick reputation. It wouldn't have mattered that I was bleeding like a stuck pig. Killing me is killing me."

She drew back her shoulders. "Yes, I suppose it would be quite an accomplishment to shoot the fastest gun west of the Mississippi."

With difficulty, he rolled his head from side to side. He didn't know why he wanted her to understand, but it seemed important that she know the truth—or at least part of it. "I'm not fast at all."

"Then how in heaven's name did you gain your reputation?"

"I'm deadly accurate."

She bolted from the bed, the movement jarring his shoulder, sending shards of agony ricocheting through it. Groaning low, he slammed his eyes closed and gritted his teeth, waiting for the wave of pain to ease. He concentrated on the steady staccato beat of her heels as she paced the floor. In each step, he heard the anger, frustration, and disappointment. Then the pacing came to an abrupt stop. He opened his eyes, knowing what she would say before she spoke the words.

"As soon as you're strong enough, I want you off my property."

She strode from the room in a flurry of whispering skirts. He sank further into the softness of the bed. The pain had shifted from his shoulder to his heart, the incredible ache almost unbearable.

But he would bear it as he had since he was fourteen. He'd live with the agony, the guilt, and the loneliness . . . until the day that he came upon a man who was more accurate than he was.

Closing his eyes, he drifted into the welcome oblivion where the past was merely a shrouded mist.

"Is HE GONNA die, Lil?" Toby asked.

Lillian studied the man lying in her bed. When he

awoke earlier, she'd thought he was well on his way to recovery. Now she wasn't so sure. Although his fever was raging, he was shivering as though he'd just emerged from a river in winter. "I don't know," she whispered as she dipped a cloth into a bowl of warm water. She wrung it out and began to wipe the sweat from his throat. She felt his body stiffen beneath her fingers.

"Don't go for the gun," he rasped. "Goddamn it! Don't go for the gun!"

He jerked, kicking at the blankets. She pressed her hands to his shoulders. "Mr. Wilder?" His breath came in short little gasps. "Mr. Wilder?"

"He's gonna draw, dammit!" Groaning low, he convulsed, waving his hand frantically. She wrapped her hand tightly around his, and he settled into stillness. His breathing slowly evened out and he opened his eyes. She saw pain reflected in his silver depths, pain that traveled clear to his soul. "He's dead," he whispered.

It wasn't a question, but she nodded anyway.

"I didn't want to kill him," he said, his voice low.

Then why did you? hung on the tip of her tongue, but she couldn't bring herself to voice her true thoughts when he seemed so weak, struggling with his inner turmoil.

"I know," she said softly, not fully understanding why she needed to comfort this man who was clinging to her hand as though it was the only thing keeping him anchored in this world. She felt him relax as though her words gave him absolution. She leaned forward. "Mr. Wilder, do you have family? Is there someone I should notify if you should . . . should die?"

He rolled his head from side to side. "No family. No one who cares." He smiled, reminding her of a small boy about to play a prank. "I won't die in your bed, lady."

Her stomach lurched. Her troubles began the night Jack Ward had died in her bed. "See that you don't."

His eyes drifted closed, but his hand remained firmly wrapped around hers. He had stopped shivering, and his cheeks felt a little cooler to her touch. She sat on the bed and stared at their clasped hands. He was a killer, but for a few moments he had simply been a man haunted by demons. She wished she hadn't witnessed his vulnerability—wished she hadn't wanted to hold him close and make the pain go away.

CHANCE AWOKE EXHAUSTED, his shoulder aching. Shafts of sunlight pierced the room. A woman's room. It carried the fading fragrance of roses in bloom. Turning his head slightly, he saw the boy standing beside the bed, reverently touching the harmonica that rested on the bedside table.

"Do you—" He'd planned to ask the boy if he knew how to play, but he couldn't push the words past his parched throat.

The boy jerked his head around. "Bet you're needing some water," he announced with authority.

Chance struggled to sit up as the boy poured water from an earthen pitcher into a glass. He felt weaker than a newborn babe. He took the offered glass, hating the way his hand shook as he gingerly sipped on the cool liquid that eased the ache in his throat. Over the rim of the glass, he studied the one responsible for his current predicament. The boy no longer had cotton stuffed up his nose, but an ugly black bruise framed one eye. "Your nose hurting?"

The boy shook his head vigorously. "Lil said it'll probably be somewhat crooked, but that it'll give me character."

Chance couldn't prevent a corner of his mouth from lifting. "Character, huh?"

The boy nodded. "I reckon that's a good thing to have—whatever it is."

Chance's smile grew. "Not too many people have character these days."

"Do you?"

His smile withered away. "None at all."

"I'm supposed to get Lil if you woke up," he said, and hightailed it out of the room.

Breathing heavily, Chance sank against the pillow and rested the glass on his bare chest.

Wiping her hands on a crisp white apron, the woman strolled boldly into the room, seemingly not at all fearful of his reputation. Her fiery hair was caught up in a braid that draped over one shoulder. "You're awake."

"You say that like you had doubts."

"You ran a fever for two days."

Shock rippled through him. "Two days? What day is it?"

"Thursday."

"I need my clothes," he barked.

"You need to rest," she insisted.

Fighting not to appear as weak as he felt, he started to sit up. "I need to get some fresh air, start gathering my strength—"

She pushed him down with one hand pressed against his uninjured shoulder. "Let me feed you some broth first."

"Where's my gun?"

"I put it away."

"Get it."

"You're not in any danger."

"Lady, the only time I don't wear a gun is when I'm making love to a woman, so unless you're aiming to climb into this bed with me, bring me the damn gun."

Fire flashed within the blue depths of her eyes. She stomped to the bureau, jerked open the top drawer, and snatched out his gun belt. She stalked to the bed and flung it at him. Groaning when it thudded against his chest, he grabbed the holster and closed his hand around the smooth handle of the Colt, welcoming the uncomfortable peace it always brought him. He captured her gaze, certain she wanted to tell him exactly what he could do with his gun: use it on himself. Not that he hadn't once contemplated it. "Does anyone know I'm hurt?"

"No. I considered going for a doctor yesterday evening when you were delirious, but you threatened to put a bullet between my eyes if I did."

He nodded. "The boy?"

"Hasn't left your side."

In her voice, he heard the anger seething beneath the

surface. He couldn't fault her. "I'll eat now," he said quietly.

Her fists swinging at her sides she stormed from the room. Lord, she was mostly spit, but she intrigued him. He couldn't recall the last time a woman had caught his fancy.

He slid his gaze over to the boy, who furrowed his brow. "You wouldn't really have killed her, would you?"

Chance slowly shook his head. "Nope. But in my line of work, you live longer if people believe the lies."

Chapter 3

As THE LOW haunting melody of a harmonica filled the late afternoon air, Lillian stepped out of the barn where she'd been tending to the cows. Chance Wilder sat on the porch, his back against the wall, the front legs of the wooden straight-backed chair in the air, the harmonica pressed to his lips.

Toby sat beside him, his chair in the same reclining position, his eyes fastened on Wilder with something akin to adoration.

Reluctantly she had to admit she'd been impressed by Wilder's determination to summon up the strength to make his way to the front porch. His jaw had been clenched against the pain, his movements slow and measured as he shuffled through the house. He didn't comment on the sparse, simple furnishings, although she suspected he was more focused on moving one foot in front of the other instead of his surroundings. Once he reached his destination, he sat there all afternoon, Toby pestering him with one question after another, which he patiently answered, although he never volunteered more information than was needed to appease her brother's curiosity. She realized now that his impatience the first day had been the result of his directing all his efforts toward staying on his horse.

She didn't like witnessing his tolerance. It was much easier to dislike him when he was short-tempered with Toby. Much easier to dislike him before she'd seen his vulnerability and held his hand through the night.

She strolled to the house and rested her arms on the porch railing. The slight breeze toyed with the curls circling Wilder's head. His mouth moved slowly over the instrument, and she imagined his lips trailing a path along her throat. Heat that had little to do with late summer surged through her.

As though reading her thoughts, Wilder paused in playing and lifted a corner of his mouth. "Evenin'."

Her heart thundered as though she'd never had a man speak to her with a sparkle in his eyes. "Toby, you need to finish up your chores before supper," she announced, fighting to ignore the blatant attraction she felt for this man, this hired killer. She couldn't explain it, much less understand it. He represented violence when all she desperately longed for was peace.

"Ah, Lil—"

"Do what your sister says," Wilder ordered.

With a scowl, Toby dropped the chair onto all fours and tromped toward the barn.

"Don't take offense, Mr. Wilder, but I'd rather you didn't encourage him—"

"Encourage him to do what? His chores?" he asked.

"Encourage him to spend time in your company. He's at an age where he's easily swayed. I'd rather he not be influenced by a man who kills."

"You'd rather he be influenced by an old man's whore?"

Lillian staggered back as though he'd slapped her. Humiliation swamped her, angered her—that this sinner should sit in judgment of her. "What Jack Ward was to me is none of your damn business!"

Chance watched her storm past him and disappear into the house. He cursed long and hard under his breath. He had no right to say what he had, but every time he thought of an old man's gnarled hands touching her, touching her the way he wanted to, the way she'd never let him . . .

The boy loped to the house, his smile bright. Chance was surprised the kid's jaw didn't ache as a result of his constant grins. He leapt onto the porch. "You comin' in for supper?"

"Think I'll stay outside a little longer. Smells like your sister cooked up some stew. Why don't you bring me a bowl?"

"I'll sit out here with you," he offered.

Chance shook his head. "Your sister needs the company."

The boy nodded reluctantly before going inside. Chance slipped the harmonica into his pocket and gazed toward the horizon. Evening would arrive soon. In the passing years, he had most missed sitting on a porch in the quiet after a day filled with exhausting work. Now when his body ached, it was more often from a bullet wound than from laboring in the fields. In the evening, his back was usually against a wall in a saloon, while he drank whiskey, hoping to dull the memories and the yearning for a life far different than the one he led.

Hearing the footsteps, he glanced back over his shoulder. The woman stood in the doorway, a wooden bowl in her hands. "Toby said you wanted to eat out here."

"Thought it best."

She gave him a brusque nod, handed him the bowl, and turned to go back inside.

"Miss Madison?"

She stopped, but didn't look at him.

"I owe you an apology. I had no right to say what I did."

She met and held his gaze, a corner of her mouth lifting slightly. "Well, we finally agree on something."

"We agree on something else. I won't be influencing the boy. I'll leave come morning."

Her smile fell and she furrowed her brow. "You can't be fully recovered."

"Thanks to your tender ministrations, I'm strong enough. I'll bed down in the barn tonight and be gone by first light."

"When you're finished eating, come inside and I'll change your bandage."

He waited until she went into the house. Then he lifted

the bowl of stew, inhaled the spicy aromas, and knew a longing so intense that he nearly doubled over with it.

He missed all the things he'd never have: meals prepared by a woman with loving care, a home where he could sit in the middle of the room, children who looked up to him . . . and a woman who loved him.

LILLIAN CURSED HER shaking hands as she unwound the bandages from around Chance Wilder's shoulder as he sat on the bed in her room. Her gaze slipped lower. A fine sprinkling of hair covered his chest. Tenderly, she touched her fingers to the wound and felt him stiffen. "I'm sorry. I just want to make certain no infection is brewing. You're really fortunate that the bullet went clean through."

"Yep."

She'd had to dig out some bits of cloth, but thankfully no lead. Her fingers strayed to a scar on his shoulder, the remnants of another wound. Other scars marked his arm. "Do you always get shot in a gunfight?"

"I usually come away with a nick or two. Like I said, I'm not fast."

"Then why do you do it?"

"Why do you stay here when you're not wanted?"

Her fingers stilled as she studied his eyes. Silver like the gun he wore. She reached for clean bandages and began to redress the wound. "I have my reasons," she stated softly.

"And I have mine."

He bit back a groan when she jerked the bandage into

a knot. "But you kill!" she spat, loathing laced through her voice.

"You wanted him to rape you?"

Horrified at the callousness of his words, the ease with which he spoke of such brutality, she stepped back. "No, but you could have wounded him."

He gave a long thoughtful nod. "Could have."

"You should have. Wounding him would have stopped him as effectively as killing him."

"Would have stopped him this week. But what about the next? Or the one after that? You protest and act disgusted as though I killed an innocent man. One of his boys held a gun to your brother's temple. You think he wouldn't have given the order to shoot?"

Pressing a hand to her mouth, she spun around. Yes, he would have killed her brother to gain what he wanted from her. She pivoted back around. "Who are you to be judge, jury, and executioner?"

"He knew my reputation. He drew first. If I'd wounded him, he would have come after me, and he would have seen to it the odds weren't so even because then it would have been a matter of revenge. I learned the hard way to never leave a man who drew on me breathing, because he'll find another time to draw on me—usually when my back is turned."

"How can you live like that?"

Averting his gaze, he stood and reached for his shirt, but not before she caught a glimpse of loneliness reflected in his eyes. Grunting with his efforts, he pulled his shirt over his head. Without thought, she tugged the linen down and began to slip the buttons into place. She felt the touch of his gaze roaming over her face like a gentle caress. She didn't move when he slowly lifted his hand. Tenderly, he cradled her cheek with a roughened palm that killed. She raised her eyes to his.

"I remember you holding my hand, caressing my brow—"

"I'd caress a snake to keep it from dying in my bed."

His unexpected smile sent unwanted shafts of pleasure swirling through her. It changed him, made him look not so harsh, made it easy to forget that he valued life so little.

"You know the legend, lady, but you don't know the man. And damn if I'm not tempted to introduce you to the man."

His nostrils flared, his lips parted as he lowered his mouth. She knew she should step away, but her feet were rooted to the spot like an ancient oak tree. He was wild and dangerous, everything she feared, all that she longed for. She welcomed the strength in his hand as he tilted her face, the yearning in his silver eyes, his breath wafting over her cheek as he neared.

Thundering footsteps resounded through the house mere seconds before Toby burst into the room. "Riders are comin'!"

Tenseness rippled through Wilder as he pierced her with his narrowed, suspicious gaze. She shook her head, knowing by his guarded expression what he was thinking. "I didn't tell anyone you were hurt."

He snapped his attention to Toby. "How many?"

"They're workin' up a cloud of dust. I couldn't count 'em."

Chance released her, withdrew his gun with the hand that had just caressed her cheek, checked the bullets, and slipped it back into his holster. He grabbed his duster, grimacing as he maneuvered into it. He settled his hat low over his brow. "You and the boy stay inside. If bullets start to fly, take cover."

"Not every person is a threat."

"If I'm wrong, then you can invite them in for tea," he growled as he stalked from the room. She heard the front door slam in his wake.

"I don't think he's wrong, Lil," Toby said.

She slipped her arm around him. "You stay here. I'm going into the front room so I can see what's happening." As quietly as possible she left her bedroom, crept to the window that overlooked the porch, eased the blue gingham curtains aside and peered out. Wilder stood on the front porch, one hip cocked, his duster pulled back to reveal his gun. The riders drew their horses to a halt. One man urged his mount forward.

"Are you Chance Wilder?"

"Yep." Wilder pulled a matchstick from his pocket and wedged it between his teeth.

"They say you always work for the man with the best offer."

"That's what they say," Wilder replied.

"Mr. Ward wants to see you up at his house."

Wilder withdrew the match from his mouth and

pointed toward the corral. "I'd be obliged if one of your men would saddle my horse. It's the dun-colored beauty."

Lillian sank to the floor, her heart thundering. She could think of only one reason why John Ward would seek an audience with Chance Wilder. He wanted to hire the man, and she knew he'd offer Wilder more than a harmonica, a bent coin, and a length of string.

CHANCE'S SPURS JANGLED as he followed John Ward's foreman through the sprawling ranch house to a room decorated with cow skulls and horns. A man in his mid-thirties glanced up from his chair behind a large oak desk. "Come in, Mr. Wilder, and have a seat."

Ignoring the chair set in front of the desk, Chance ambled to a leather chair that rested against the wall. He sat and casually crossed his foot over his knee, studying the man who was studying him. John Ward looked as though he'd earned his place in the world.

"You're dismissed," he said to the foreman without taking his gaze off Chance. The foreman backed out of the room and closed the door behind him.

"You were supposed to meet with me this afternoon," Ward said.

"Had something else to do."

A muscle twitched in Ward's jaw. "Wade Armstrong worked for me." He leaned forward. "I thought you did, too."

"I got a better offer."

Ward narrowed his blue eyes and set his mouth into a grim line. "I don't take kindly to being betrayed. You and I had an understanding."

"I never commit myself to an offer until I get a lay of the land and a feel for the stakes involved. I spent two days riding your land. I can't see that it's hurting you not to have that little patch the woman's living on."

"How in the hell do you think my mother feels knowing that her husband died in his whore's bed?"

Chance's stomach knotted. Jack Ward had died in Lillian's bed, in her arms? Something akin to jealousy shot through him at the thought. He knew what she was, but he hadn't truly envisioned her in bed with the man, in the bed in which she'd tended his wound. "Make her an offer—"

"My father gave her all she'll ever get from the Wards. I want her and the boy run off that land, and if you won't do it, I'll find someone who will."

"Be sure that he's as good as his reputation because he'll have to get past me first." Chance unfolded his body and strode from the room.

Chapter 4

WITH TREMBLING HANDS, Lillian dunked the plate into the bucket of hot water. Wilder had returned earlier, dismounted, and sank to the porch. He'd ordered Toby to see after his horse. She wanted to tell him to get back on his horse and ride out, but he'd gripped the railing post so tightly that his knuckles turned white, and she realized he wasn't nearly as recovered as he'd led her to believe. His face had dripped sweat, and she'd seen the small tremors racking his body. She would have offered to help him if he hadn't given her a steely glare. It was several long moments before he was finally able to pull himself to his feet and deposit his body in the chair on the porch.

Frustrated, she returned to the kitchen to wash the dishes she'd let soak while he was gone. She heard Toby's excited voice. He'd no doubt finished tending to the horse.

She set the last dish aside. Wiping her hands on her

apron, she walked quietly to the front doorway and gazed out. With three fingers curled against his palm, Toby pointed one finger and raised his thumb in the air.

"Pow! Pow!" he cried, flinging himself to the ground and rolling like he'd seen the gunman do that first day in Lonesome. He jumped to his feet, a wide grin splitting his freckled face in two. "They didn't shoot today 'cuz they was scared of you," he said.

"They weren't scared of me, boy. They were scared of death," Wilder drawled.

"When I grow up, I'm gonna be just like you," Toby said, his face beaming.

Lillian's throat tightened. She wanted Toby to have the influence of a man in his life, but not when that man was a cold-stone murderer.

"You don't want that, boy," Wilder said, and Lillian suddenly realized that he never called Toby by name.

"Sure I do," Toby said, easing nearer to the porch, his head bobbing. "I'll be famous—"

"What you'll be . . . is staring down the road at a long stretch of lonesome," Wilder said, his voice a deep rumble, but in the midst of it, Lillian thought she heard a sigh of regret.

She stepped onto the porch. Wilder slid his gaze over to her. He'd removed his hat and the slight breeze toyed with the soft curls. Moving past him, she dropped onto the top step and regarded the horizon where the sun painted its farewell tapestry.

"Where do you live?" Toby asked, inching forward on the balls of his feet.

"Under the stars."

"Ain't you got a house somewheres?"

"Nope."

Toby darted a quick glance at Lillian before looking back at Wilder. She knew that her brother had always longed for a house instead of a room over a saloon. His dream brought her here, kept her here even when everyone wanted her to leave, even when she knew it would be so much easier to go.

"How 'bout kids? You got kids?" Toby asked.

"None that I know of."

Lillian felt the heat warm her cheeks as the image of this man in bed with a woman fluttered through her mind and took root. He wouldn't be wearing his gun . . . or anything else for that matter. "Toby, you need to stop pestering Mr. Wilder."

"I ain't pesterin' him," Toby protested. He angled his head and studied Wilder. "Am I?"

Wilder shot a look at Lillian, and she realized she'd dug herself into a hole. She'd asked him not to encourage Toby. To fulfill her request, he'd have to hurt Toby's feelings and tell him that he was a nuisance. Wilder squinted into the distance. "I'm just a little tuckered out."

"On account of you bein' shot?" Toby asked.

"Yeah."

Toby sat next to her. Digging his bony elbows into his skinny thighs, he leaned forward with a deep sigh to watch the sunset. Lillian turned to thank Wilder for sparing Toby's feelings. A knot formed in her chest at the raw tenderness she saw reflected in his eyes just before he averted his attention away from her brother and stared again at the horizon. The loneliness he'd mentioned to Toby earlier was wrapped around him like a shroud. What would it be like to have no home, no family? As hard as things had been growing up, she'd always had the love of her mother, and now Toby's unfettered devotion.

"Is your shoulder hurting?" she asked.

Remaining focused on the distance, he shook his head slightly. "Aches a little."

"Maybe we should put your arm in a sling, to ease the pressure on your wound."

He slid his penetrating, silvered gaze over to her. "It's best not to care, lady."

She turned away, allowing the silence between them to thicken, the chasm to widen. The man who wore his reputation seemed so different from the one sitting on her front porch. She had not expected tenderness from a killer or a showing of respect for her wishes. He had never harmed her or Toby, but she couldn't overlook the fact that he had hurt others.

"Beautiful sunset," he said quietly, with reverence.

Lillian snapped her head around, unable to keep the surprise from reflecting in her voice. "I didn't expect you to be a man who would notice—"

"I notice everything, lady. It's what's kept me alive." He leaned the chair back, resting his head against the wall. "Boy, if you decide to follow the path I've tread, you'll need to learn that."

Toby swiveled his head around. "Learn what?"

"To appreciate every minute you're given. You never know which one will be your last."

Toby furrowed his young brow. "I figure the last one will come during a gunfight."

"The last one will come when you don't expect it, when your back isn't against a wall."

"You think someone would shoot you in the back?" Lillian asked.

He shrugged.

"How can you live always expecting to die?"

"If I expect it, maybe it'll be longer in coming."

"And what do you gain?"

"Another sunset."

She turned away, not certain what to make of this man. Then Wilder began to play the harmonica. Its lowly strains floated around her, a seductive melody echoing loneliness. She felt a strong urge to reach out to him, but he'd chosen his path. The music faded into the silence as the sun disappeared and darkness blanketed the land.

"Where did you get the mouth organ, boy?" Wilder asked.

Toby twisted around. "It belonged to my pa. He carried it with him during the war."

"Where is he now?"

"Dead."

Lillian wished that the night hadn't turned Wilder into little more than a silhouette. She wanted to see his face, to know what he was thinking as he held her brother's precious gift.

"What about the string?"

"Nothing special about it. Just figured you never know when you'll need a length of string so decided it was a good thing to carry about. But the penny is a lucky penny. I put it on a railroad track and a train ran over it."

"You're lucky the train didn't run over you," he said.

"That's what Lil said. That's why it's a lucky penny."

Lillian heard Wilder's low chuckle. She stared through the darkness. She *had* said those exact words to Toby. The knowledge that she and Wilder would have similar thoughts unsettled her. She rubbed Toby's shoulder. "Need to get yourself ready for bed."

"But it ain't late."

"It's late enough for you."

With a disgusted sigh, he scrambled to his feet and onto the porch.

"Here, boy."

In the shadows, she was able to make out Wilder extending the harmonica.

"That's yours now," Toby told him.

"I figure I'm alive because you talked your sister into tending my shoulder. This is payment."

Toby snatched it out of his hand and held the harmonica to his mouth. His quick burst of air sent a squeaky noise into the night. As he walked into the house, more followed.

"He's a good kid," Wilder said quietly.

"He has a name," she snapped. "It's Toby."

"You call a person by name, it makes it harder to forget him."

"What about the people you killed? Did you know their names?"

"Some of them."

She moved her feet up to the next step and wrapped her arms around her drawn-up knees. She thought she might actually like the man if he had chosen a different occupation. "How much was Ward going to pay you?" she asked softly. When his answer was silence, she glanced over her shoulder, pinning him with a glare. "He is the one who brought you to Lonesome, isn't he?"

"No, lady. You're the one who brought me to Lonesome."

Her heart pounded frantically against her ribs with the confirmation that she was the person he'd come to kill. "How much did he offer?"

"Ten thousand," he said quietly.

"That's a lot of money."

"Sure is, and he's gonna offer it to someone else. Whether you want to admit it or not, lady, you need me."

"I don't need you. We have a sheriff who is paid to protect the citizens of Lonesome."

"And where was he the other day?"

Unexpectedly in need of comfort, she hugged herself as she struggled to find an explanation for the sheriff's absence. Surely he wasn't abandoning her as well. She'd broken no laws. "Maybe he was busy with other business, but I plan to speak with him tomorrow about John Ward and his threats. I should have done it sooner but I honestly didn't think he'd take things this far."

"I'll go with you."

"You said you were leaving in the morning."

"I'll leave as soon as you've talked with the sheriff."

She heard the hushed click of the chair hitting the porch as though it were as weary as the man who sat in it. His boots reverberated over the porch and thudded on the step. She jerked her head up.

"Night," he said as he hit the ground.

She shot to her feet. "No."

He stopped, turned, and took a step back toward her. "No?"

She licked her suddenly parched lips. "I . . . I just don't think it's a good idea for you to sleep in the barn. You increase the chances of your wound getting infected."

"Figured you'd prefer for me to be out of the house."

She nodded, trying to understand why she didn't just let him go. Maybe it was the manners her mother had bred into her, or more likely, it was the fact that he had kept his word to Toby and was still watching out for her. "If John Ward should come back tonight—"

"He won't."

"How do you know?"

"He hasn't had time to hire my replacement, and he's not about to risk his life until he feels like he's got someone to cover his back." He took a step closer, and she watched the moonlight play over his golden hair. "Why do you want me in the house?"

"As payment," she blurted, the heat flaming her face. "Payment for your kindness to Toby . . . and for saving me. I hate that you killed the man—" Tears burned the back of her eyes. She despised the weakness that made her sink back onto the porch steps. She wrapped her arms around herself and rocked back and forth, memories of the glittering lust and hatred burning in Wade's eyes assailing her. "He was going . . . going to . . . no one would stop him."

Wilder's strong arms suddenly embraced her as he joined her on the step and held her near. She pressed her head against his warm, sturdy chest and heard the constant thudding of his heart.

"No one wants you here. Why don't you leave?" he asked in a low rumble.

She shook her head. "This place was the only gift Jack Ward ever gave me. It's special to me."

"You loved him?" he asked quietly.

She nodded her head jerkily. "I shouldn't have. God knows I should have despised him, but I never could bring myself to hate him. Even now when his gift brings me such pain, I can't overlook the fact that he gave it to me out of love."

"Have you ever talked with John Ward, tried to settle the differences?"

"No. John came here one night with an army of men. He told me to pack up and get, then threatened to kill me as a trespasser if I ever set foot on his land. Delivered his message and rode out. Makes it hard to reason with a man when you can't get near him."

"It's even harder to reason with him if he's dead."

Lillian's heart slammed against her ribs. Trembling, she clutched Wilder's shirt and lifted her head from his chest, trying to see into the depths of his silver eyes, but they were only shadows hidden by the night. His embrace was steady, secure, his hands slowly trailing up and down her back. "Promise me you won't kill him," she demanded.

A silence stretched between them as though he were weighing the promise against the offer that he'd cloaked as a simple statement. "If he's dead, you and the boy will be safe."

She tightened her fingers around his shirt and gave him a small shake. "I don't want the blood of Jack Ward's son on my hands. Give me your word that you won't kill him."

His hands stilled. "What are you willing to pay me to keep me from killing him?"

Her stomach knotted, her chest ached with a tightness that threatened to suffocate her. Even though she couldn't see it clearly, she felt the intensity of his perusal. She had no money, nothing to offer him—nothing to offer a killer except herself. And she knew that he was aware of that fact.

Had she actually begun to feel sympathy for this man whose solitary life gave him no roots, allowed him no love? He was worse than Wade because at least Wade had barreled into her, announcing loudly and clearly what he wanted of her. The killer wanted the same thing, but he'd lured her into caring for him and trusting him, catching her heart unawares.

The pain of betrayal ripped through her, and she thought she might actually understand why one man would kill another. Tiny shudders coursed through her body and tears stung her eyes as she answered hoarsely, "I'll pay anything."

Beneath her clutched hand, his heart increased its tempo, pounding harder and faster. He cradled her face between his powerful hands. "Anything?" he whispered. "If I want all a woman can offer?"

She nodded jerkily. "I don't want John Ward killed." How could she warn the man when approaching him meant her certain death?

Wilder leaned in until his warm breath fanned her face. He shifted his thumbs and gently stroked the corners of her mouth. "I give you my word that I'll let the bastard live."

He slashed his mouth over hers, demanding, claiming all that she offered to willingly pay: her body, her heart, her soul. She could not give one without giving the others.

His tongue delved deeply, hungrily, as though he were a man coming off a fast. Then like a man whose hunger had eased, he gentled his touch. He threaded his fingers through her hair while the callused pads of his thumbs caressed her cheek. She had never been kissed with such tenderness, had never experienced so great a yearning to give back in kind what she was receiving. She twined her arms around his neck and heard his guttural groan. He tore his mouth from hers and blazed a trail of hot, moist kisses along the column of her throat. A tiny gasp escaped her lips.

Without warning, he surged to his feet. She stared at his rigid back and listened to his harsh breathing echoing through the night. She struggled to her feet. Afraid her trembling legs would give out beneath her, she clung to the porch post for support. "Chance?"

"Go to bed, Li—lady," he growled.

She licked her swollen lips, tasting where he had been. "Are you—"

"I'm sleeping in the barn."

"I don't understand. I thought you wanted me."

He spun around. "Christ, lady, I do want you . . . more than I've ever wanted anything. And that's the very reason I won't take what you're offering."

She watched him storm toward the barn, disappointment slamming into her. Disappointment with him because he'd left her with a woman's yearnings. Disappointment with herself because she wished he'd satisfied those longings.

Chapter 5

HAVING ENDURED A restless night's sleep, Lillian dragged herself out of bed before the sun had yet to peer over the horizon. After washing her face, brushing and rebraiding her hair, she changed into a simple dress and apron. She made her bed, then walked to the window. Wilder's horse was still in the corral. She was hoping that he might have left sometime during the night. It was going to be awkward to greet him this morning. She had difficulty believing what she'd offered him. Or the sting of mortification she'd felt when he rejected it.

She couldn't deny that Wilder was handsome in a rugged sort of way. Nor could she deny that she was drawn to him as she'd never been drawn to another man. Maybe it was the loneliness in him that so mirrored hers. Maybe it was because they were both outcasts. Maybe it was because in spite of his roughened manner, he was patient with Toby.

Or maybe it was simply that he would be leaving soon, taking with him the absence of judgment. He didn't look at her as though she were beneath him. He didn't talk to her condescendingly. He didn't turn his back on her. He didn't try to harm her.

None of those things could be said about the citizens of this area. They were never going to accept her, not if John Ward had any say in the matter, and it appeared he had a great deal of say. But she wasn't going to be run off. The land was hers, and by God, they could bury her in it, but they weren't going to take it from her.

Sighing, she contemplated the barn inside which Wilder slept. She couldn't leave the cows much longer without milking them. No reason for them to suffer simply because she was dreading seeing the man who had kissed her so thoroughly and then walked away.

Grabbing the lamp, she left her room and peered into Toby's. He was still sprawled over the bed. He got up with the sun, not before. She refrained from going in and ruffling her fingers through his hair. She didn't know if she'd ever love anyone as much as she loved him. She hated that he was so quickly losing his innocence. Maybe they should leave, but what would she be teaching him if they walked away simply because things were difficult? If she'd learned one lesson in life, it was that things were always challenging.

In the kitchen, she traded the lamp for a lantern. When she stepped onto the porch, she realized the barn door was ajar and pale light was spilling out into the graying dawn. Straining her ears to hear any sounds coming from inside, she heard only the gentle wind whistling through the trees. With the lantern held aloft to guide her steps, she made her way to the sturdy structure. As silently as possible, she eased through the opening and was greeted with the low hum of her favorite song, "Red River Valley," and the *shoosh* of milk hitting tin. She tip-toed forward until she reached Bessie's far stall.

Wilder sat on a small stool that was too short for his long legs. His hands were busy working Bessie's teats. He wore only his shirt, trousers, boots, and gun. But for a moment he appeared almost peaceful, lost in the perpetual rhythm, humming, eyes closed. She wanted to kneel beside him, comb her fingers through his hair, trail her thumbs over his face, settle them at the corners of his mouth.

But he seemed so serene, she felt like an intruder. Yet she couldn't make herself walk away. She wondered what had put this man on the path he traveled. He didn't seem evil or wicked or mean.

Bessie mooed. Wilder slowly opened his eyes. "Had your fill of staring?" he asked.

"I wasn't staring." That would be rude. "I was just caught off-guard. How long have you known I was here?"

"Since you walked through the door."

"You could have said something."

He peered over at her, a corner of his mouth hitching up. "So could you."

She wasn't going to confess she'd been too entranced, that he was a contradiction she wanted to explore, even knowing that with him, there would never be anything beyond heartache. "I don't expect you to do my chores."

"It's good exercise for my hands, keeps them loose. I would have chopped some firewood for you, but I don't think my shoulder is up to heaving an ax just yet."

She thought of how welcome it would be to have a man around permanently to handle that difficult task for her.

"Why doesn't the boy see to this chore?" he asked. "I was milking cows at his age."

Suddenly he looked uncomfortable, as though he'd revealed too much. She'd never envisioned him as a child. Milking a cow seemed a normal activity for a boy. She wondered what else he might have done: swam in the creek, climbed trees, chased butterflies. No, she couldn't see him doing the latter. That was an activity in which she'd engaged, wanting to hold something so pretty. Instead she'd squashed one of the delicate creatures in her enthusiasm and never chased another. "I don't like him being out here before the sun is up. You never know what sort of animal is lurking in the shadows."

His expression hardened, and she was compelled to say, "I wasn't referring to you."

Yesterday morning, she would have been, but now she didn't know what to make of him.

"You can't protect him forever," he said.

"No, but I can for a while."

His hands stilled. Reaching for the bucket, he stood.

"I can carry that to the house," she told him.

"I'll do it. It'll be good for my shoulder. It's getting stiff."

The sun was beginning to ease over the horizon, hinting at a lovely day. She doused the flame in the lantern and tried not to consider the manner in which he barely looked at her. For all of his attitude, the kiss last night might just as well not have happened. It irritated her that she could grow warm with his nearness while he seemed not at all affected by hers.

She fought not to think about what it might be like to walk beside a man every morning as they tended to chores. She'd never had fanciful thoughts about love. She was much too practical. But sometimes . . .

"Do you ever think about settling down, Mr. Wilder?"

"No point in it."

"In thinking about it or settling down?" she asked, making her voice light.

"Both. I see no point in longing for what you can't have."

"Surely as big as this country is, you could find a place where people wouldn't seek you out."

"You're going on the assumption that I don't want to be found."

She nearly staggered over her feet, with the certain realization that he chose this life of violence. How easy it was to forget as a new dawn brought brightness to the day that darkness still hovered.

He set the bucket on the porch. "Let me know when you're ready to head into town. I'll saddle a horse for you." He turned on his heel.

It seemed in this matter, at least, Wilder was going to serve as her champion, apparently holding with his promise to escort her to the sheriff. Her father had never been present when she was growing up, Toby's father had been in their lives only briefly, so she'd never known what it was to rely on a man for protection. She was accustomed to being independent, standing up for herself. Still, reluctantly she admitted that she was grateful she wouldn't have to go into town alone. She needed to put her reservations about this man aside and show her gratitude. "Breakfast will be on the table in half an hour, Mr. Wilder. I expect you not to be tardy."

Stopping, he looked back over his shoulder. "Appreciate the food. I'll take it on the porch."

"The table, Mr. Wilder. Inside."

He lifted his arm, fingers poised as though to touch the brim of a hat he suddenly realized he wasn't wearing. "I'll wash up."

Lifting the bucket, she watched as his long strides carried him back to the barn. He'd be leaving after they saw the sheriff. She didn't know why she wanted him to carry the memory of a few more minutes in her company with him. Or why she wanted to pretend for a while that neither of them were pariahs.

CHANCE COULDN'T REMEMBER the last time he sat down to a meal at a table situated inside a house. He ate in saloons, the occasional hotel, sitting in front of a campfire beneath the stars. And on front porches. He didn't usually get invited inside someone's home. He didn't count waking up in her bedroom. No invitation had been issued. Necessity had led him there.

But this . . . standing close to the table that was set

near an oven, he watched as she bent over and removed biscuits from the heated interior. He grew warm at the sight of her backside, the apron strings running along a curve he longed to touch. He should have told her she couldn't order him to eat at her table. He should have just mounted his horse and ridden out. But where she was concerned, he hadn't done what he should since the boy barreled into the saloon asking for his help.

"Is there anything I can see to?" he asked.

"Just have a seat," she said, smiling at him as she set down a basket holding the biscuits. A small bit of flour rested on the curve of her cheek, right up against her nose. He wanted to wipe it away with his lips, then take his mouth on a journey that covered every inch of her.

He'd known the moment she stepped into the barn. He'd trained himself to be attuned to his environment, to sense changes, to be alert to the smallest fluctuation in his surroundings. He'd heard the crinkle of hay beneath her feet, felt the shift in air accommodating her movements, was aware of her soft short breaths. When she was near enough, he inhaled her fragrance. He'd sat on that stool relishing the ordinary, had allowed those quiet moments to carry him back to a time before he'd strapped on a gun, when he would have welcomed her into his arms and greeted the day with far more passion.

Dangerous to let his thoughts wander to the possibilities that might exist between them. He couldn't stay and she didn't want to leave. And even if she did, what could he offer except the opportunity to watch him die when his luck ran out?

"Toby!" she called out, then retrieved a bowl of gravy and a plate of bacon, set them on the table, reached for her chair—

Chance beat her to it, pulling it out for her. She stared at him as though she hadn't expected him to know the courtesy a man extended to a woman. Or maybe she just thought he wouldn't have bothered, when the truth was that he wanted to do more for her. Again, dangerous thoughts that could lure him into forgetting the dangers, the loneliness, the ugliness his life entailed. He couldn't ask her to share it, wouldn't ask her.

His gaze dropped to her lips, and he contemplated taking one more kiss, just one.

The boy barreled in and dropped into his chair, breaking whatever spell had frozen them in place. She sat. Chance took his seat. She held the basket toward him.

"Lil makes the best biscuits," the boy said.

"I'm sure she does," he said, taking her offering and plucking out a biscuit that nearly scorched his fingers. He smothered it in gravy before adding the eggs and bacon to his plate. He'd wolfed down half his food before he realized she was eating slowly, delicately—civilized. "Been a while since I sat down to a meal with folks."

She smiled softly. "I take it as a testament to my cooking when it's eaten with such enthusiasm."

"Can't remember when I've had better." Returning his attention to his plate, he finished off what remained before helping himself to seconds. He figured it was the best way to compliment her.

"Toby, we'll be going to town this morning," she said.

The boy snapped his head around and stared at Chase, worry clouding blue eyes a shade lighter than his sister's. "You're coming, too, ain't you?"

Giving him a brusque nod, Chase watched as relief washed over the kid's face.

"We're going to speak with the sheriff," she said. "After that everything will be fine."

He wondered where she got her optimism. He thought it a shame that the folks around here would never give themselves the opportunity to know her. John Ward would ensure it, and he knew there was little he himself could do about it.

His plate empty, he downed the last of the sweet coffee she'd given him earlier. Then he stood. "Appreciate the meal. I'll be getting ready for our trip into town. Just let me know when you're all set to go."

He strode through the doorway and into the vast expanse of the yard. Eating in her home—and it was a home, not a house—had been a mistake. With the force of a bullet through the chest, it had reminded him of what he'd never possess. He was more determined than ever to ensure she kept it.

At any cost.

LILLIAN WAS WASHING the plates when she heard the echo of the first bullet. "Wait here," she ordered Toby.

Broom in hand after sweeping beneath the table, Toby opened his mouth to protest. Two more reports cracked the stillness of the morning.

"No arguing," she called over her shoulder, already rushing to the door. Opening it without thought to the dangers she might face, worried only about Wilder, she stepped onto the porch, surprised by the absence of men holding guns. She started to glance around—

Another gunshot. Jerking her head to the side, she saw Wilder standing a good distance from the house, his back to her, gun in holster—then the Colt was free of its moorings and he fired at a red bandana hanging from a tree branch. It whipped through the air before settling into place and fluttering in the breeze.

He slid the gun back into the holster, dragged his shirt over his head and dropped it to the ground. She watched in horror as he began removing the bandage. She started running. "Chance Wilder, don't you dare—"

She staggered to a stop as he struck with the swiftness of a rattler, sliding his gun from his holster as he went low, then froze. Breathing harshly, he shook his head. "Damn, lady, don't sneak up on a man who's practicing his shooting."

"I didn't sneak." She was having difficulty drawing in air, as though every muscle in her body had locked. "I thought you were getting ready to go to town."

He straightened, slid the gun back into the holster with ease. "I am." Rolling his shoulder, he removed the remaining bandages. The wound looked red and angry, but the stitches were holding.

"You need that linen to protect your shoulder," she told him.

"It's too confining."

Realizing with mounting dread that his readying for a trip into town included preparing himself to kill someone, she marched forward until she was standing nearly toe-to-toe with him. "I don't believe in violence, Mr. Wilder."

Staring at her as though she'd left her good sense in the kitchen, he shook his head. "It's not invisible angels that you can choose to have faith in. Violence exists, lady, whether or not you believe in it."

"You're going into town expecting trouble."

"Not expecting it, but equipped to handle it. I haven't drawn my gun in a couple of days so I need to loosen up. If you'll step aside . . ."

"And if I don't?"

He studied her as though she were a puzzle he was intent on deciphering.

She was barely aware of her fingers reaching out until they lighted upon his chest, warm and firm. She told herself that she was testing him for fever, but the fire was burning inside her, and there seemed little she could do to stop it. She felt the steady thundering of his heart against her palm. Did it remain as constant when he was facing death? "Why can't you walk away?" she asked.

Slowly he shook his head. "Damned if I know."

She wondered if he was answering a different question than what she'd intended. She wanted to know why he couldn't walk away from a gunfight. She almost convinced herself that he was saying he couldn't walk away from her.

"Do you know how to use a gun?" he asked.

"A rifle, for hunting game." She released a small laugh. "I miss my target more often than I hit it."

Stepping back, he withdrew his gun, and she worked not to regret that she was no longer touching him. He held the gun toward her. "Here, take it."

She couldn't keep the surprise from her voice. "You're giving up gunfighting?"

He grinned broadly. "No. I'm going to teach you how to use it."

"Why would I need that particular lesson?"

"Because before we visit the sheriff, we're going to the gunsmith and purchase you a pistol."

"I told you that I'm against violence."

"I'm not saying you have to use it, but nothing wrong with knowing how. And if you handle it in the shop like you know what you're doing, word will spread. Rumors alone might keep the wolves from your door. That's what you want. Just to keep them away."

She supposed there was some value in a deterrent. If she was going to have a gun on the premises, she needed to know how to use it, or at least give the impression of knowing how. Taking the gun, she was surprised by its weight and the solidness of it.

He came to stand behind her. "I assume you favor your right hand."

"Yes."

"Spread your feet, wrap both hands around the grip."

She did as he instructed. His arms came around her and his hands folded over hers. She was acutely aware of his bare chest pressed to her back, the firmness of the muscles in his arms, the strength radiating through his large hands. Lowering his head until his cheek was just a whisper's breadth from hers, he said in a low voice that sent a shiver of unwanted pleasure through her, "Using your thumbs, pull back the hammer."

She struggled with the tension, heard the click of success.

"Hold the gun level, look down the sight, aim at the center of the kerchief. You want to make it dance."

She was incredibly attuned to his nearness, his dark masculine scent, the bristles along his jaw. How could she focus on a target when all her senses were concentrated on him? "What do you know of dancing, Mr. Wilder?"

"That I'd probably step on toes."

In spite of her best intentions, she smiled. "Have you never danced?"

"No. You?"

"No." Something else they had in common. She didn't like the kinship it made her feel toward him.

"Someday a fella will dance with you."

"That sort of sentiment falls in the realm of dreams, and you don't strike me as a dreamer, Mr. Wilder."

His breathing was slow, calm, while she was hardly breathing at all. "Even a realist can occasionally have a moment's fancy."

She didn't know why his words sent joy spiraling through her. Was he imagining dancing with her, just as she was envisioning waltzing with him?

"Now, lady, aim for the red," he said in a flat voice that shattered whatever delicate connection had been weaving itself between them.

Or perhaps she was simply having a moment of insanity to believe that anything at all was developing between them. She raised the gun, looked down the length of the barrel.

"Squeeze the trigger slowly but firmly," he ordered.

She did. The flag danced. The recoil lifted her arms, knocked her back slightly, and his arms tightened around her, steadying her.

"Gawd almighty, you hit it!" Toby cried.

She and Wilder jumped apart as though they were too young lovers caught spooning. Wilder's face turned as red as an apple. The gunslinger was blushing, and that little fact warmed someplace deep inside her. She wished it didn't, wished she didn't notice everything about him. She turned to Toby. "I told you to stay in the house."

"But you were gone so long, I had to make sure you were all right."

She was at once touched and saddened that her young brother felt a responsibility toward her. She was supposed to be looking out for him.

Wilder strode to the red neckerchief and spread it wide to reveal a ragged hole. "Dang, you hit it right in the center."

He untied from the branch what she now realized was the string Toby had given him. He stuffed it and the bandana into his pocket before walking over to retrieve his gun. "Remind me to never make you mad," he said.

"I don't believe a gun is the answer to settling disputes."

"Shame John Ward doesn't feel the same. Boy, help me get the horses saddled." He snatched up his shirt and duster and headed for the barn, Toby trailing after him like a puppy desperate for a pat on the head.

It was a lucky shot, she knew that, but still, she hadn't much liked how during that one brief second when thunder had reverberated through her hands she had felt invincible. Was that what Chance Wilder was seeking? The power of life and death?

Chapter 6

"NOT A DAMN thing I can do. They haven't broken any laws."

Lillian glared at Sheriff Bergen. The graying mustache that drooped down on either side of his mouth gave him the appearance of frowning whether he was or not. She placed her hands on her hips and leaned slightly over his cluttered desk. "But he threatened to run us off our land."

"No law against threatening people." His brown eyes held an acceptance she wasn't willing to tolerate.

She leaned over farther. "He is going to hire some-one—"

"Ain't against the law to hire someone."

She jerked back. "It's not against the law to hire someone to kill me?"

The sheriff snorted. "John Ward isn't going to hire someone to kill you."

The anger surging through her, she spun around and locked her gaze onto Chance's. He stood with his back against the wall, his arms crossed over his chest, his face void of expression, as though he had expected the sheriff's words. "Didn't he offer to hire you?"

He gave a long slow nod.

"To kill me?"

He twisted his lips into a sardonic smile. "He's too smart to put it that bluntly. All he told me to do was run you off the land. A man can take that any number of ways."

"I imagine a hired killer would only take it one way," she snapped, turning her attention back to the sheriff. "You have to do something."

Bergen moved his mouth as though he were chewing an idea. "I know it's hard to understand, but until he's actually broken the law, I can't arrest him just in case he might break the law."

"This is ridiculous. Can't you at least talk to him?"

"And tell him what?" the sheriff countered. "If he kills you, I'll arrest him? He knows that."

"I can't believe there is absolutely nothing you can do."

He shook his craggy head. "My job is to enforce the law—"

"And to protect the citizens," Chance said. Lillian jerked her head around. He shifted his hard-edged gaze from her to the sheriff. "Why don't you arrange a meeting between Miss Madison and Ward? Maybe they could come to a peaceful agreement."

"I don't imagine there will be any peace unless Miss Madison leaves or John's mother dies. Mrs. Ward can't stand the thought of her husband's . . ." The deep red circles burning brightly on Sheriff Bergen's cheeks seemed out of place on the older man. He cleared his throat. ". . . Jack's mistress living near Lonesome. And you can understand if you look at it from her point of view—she was married to Jack for forty years, helped him build something out of nothing. A woman don't take kindly to evidence of a man's unfaithfulness, and him dying in your bed was damning evidence—for him and you."

Lillian tasted the bitterness of defeat. They had lived here only three months, and the happiness she and Toby longed for hovered just beyond reach. She straightened her shoulders. "Thank you for your time, Sheriff."

Trembling with fury, she marched out of the sheriff's office and stumbled to a stop on the wooden boardwalk. Toby turned away from the horses, his grin wobbly. "What'd he say?"

She forced herself to smile. "The sheriff doesn't think we have anything to worry about."

She turned her head as Chance came to stand beside her. "You knew the sheriff wouldn't do anything to help me, didn't you?" she asked, her anger smoldering.

He tugged the brim of his hat lower. "Figured there wouldn't be a lot he could do. What you need is to hire someone to protect you. Fortunately for you, your brother already did that."

"You said you were going to leave."

"Changed my mind."

Relief coursed through her, then warred with doubt. "I don't want a hired gun—"

"Don't argue with me, lady. I know you don't like what I am, but I'm the only chance you've got right now if you want to stay alive. If you won't keep me around for yourself, keep me around for the boy—until we can arrange a meeting with Ward and work out a better solution."

"I don't understand you. There's no money in this for you, there's no gain."

"Maybe there's something of more value."

"What exactly would that be?"

He looked at her so long that she didn't think he was going to answer. Finally he said, "Redemption."

A thousand questions spiraled through her mind. That he needed redeeming, she did not doubt. That helping her could provide—

"Wilder!"

She spun around. A man stood in the middle of the street, his hands flexing over a pair of guns strapped on either side of his hips. Chance slowly turned to face the man, who began to fidget.

"They say you're the best gun this side of the Rio Grande," the man announced.

Chance gave a long slow nod. "That's what they say."

"I'm calling you out."

Chance released a low sigh as he reached into his pocket, pulled out a matchstick, and wedged it between his teeth. "Lady, you and the boy get inside."

Her heart leapt into her throat. "You can't possibly—"

"Do it now," he snarled between clenched teeth.

She grabbed Toby by the arm and pulled him into the sheriff's office. With the door slamming in her wake, she scurried to the window and watched Chance saunter confidently into the middle of the street. Coming up behind her, the sheriff gazed over her shoulder. "You've got to stop them," she told him.

"Can't. They ain't broke no laws yet."

In anger, she snapped her head around so quickly she was dizzy. "Damn you! Wilder will kill him."

Sheriff Bergen shrugged easily, as though he carried no weight on those shoulders. "Probably, but Wilder always works within the law or he'd be wanted for murder."

"As long as the person who wants the killing done makes the best offer."

The sheriff raised a thick brow but didn't take his focus off the street. "Like that widow in Dripping Springs? Heard all he got from her was a pig. Besides, from what I hear, he's never killed anyone who didn't deserve to meet his Maker a little early. Take that fella who just called him out. He killed a sixteen-year-old boy in Sherman. Said he was cheating at cards. Hardly seems right to take a life over a jack of diamonds."

Gunshots cracked the air and unexpected terror ricocheted through Lillian as she swiveled her attention back to the street. Chance was walking stiffly back toward the sheriff's office, and she knew him well enough now to know he'd been wounded. The other man was sprawled in the street, his blood pooling over the ground and soaking into the earth. Grabbing Toby's hand, she rushed outside and off the boardwalk, catching up with Chance as he neared the horses, her gaze flicking wildly over him. "Where did you get shot?"

"Get on your horse," he said.

"How badly are you hurt?"

He gripped her arm and gave her a small shake, his cold eyes holding hers. "Get on the goddamn horse now." He shifted his gaze to Bergen, as the sheriff approached them. "I've got witnesses—"

"And I'm one of them," the sheriff said, stopping in front of Chance. "I saw that he drew first. His name—"

"Don't want to know his name," Chance cut in as he dropped some coins in the sheriff's palm. "See that he gets a decent burial."

Toby was already sitting astride his horse when Lillian mounted hers. She heard Chance groan low as he pulled himself into his saddle. She hoped they'd get home before he tumbled from his horse.

CHANCE WINCED AS Lillian dabbed the alcohol on his wound. The bullet had creased his right arm. The advantage to being left-handed was that his opponents had a tendency to aim for his right out of habit.

"You have got to learn to draw faster," Lillian scolded.

A corner of his mouth curved up. He couldn't remember the last time anyone had shown an ounce of concern over his well-being. "Careful, lady," he warned. "I might begin to think you care."

His stomach clenched when he saw the tears well within the depths of her blue eyes. He felt as though someone had emptied a six-gun into his chest.

"Why couldn't you have ignored him?" she rasped.

"Because he wouldn't have let up. He was in the saloon the day I got here, trying to gather the courage to challenge me. He was looking to gain a reputation. At least by facing him, I was able to control from which direction the bullet came." Cradling her cheek, stroking her soft skin, he knew he was inviting danger. Walking away last night had been the hardest thing he'd ever done—and he couldn't explain why he'd done it. She wasn't innocent. She'd been an old man's . . . lover. But never his whore. No matter how many men Lillian Madison took into her bed, she'd never be any man's whore. She was too fine, too gentle for that. So he admitted to her what he'd never told another soul. "I don't want the bullet with my name on it to come from behind."

The tears brimmed over and trailed down her cheeks, rolling along the curve of his thumb. "Is that why you always keep your back against the wall, even here?"

He nodded. "I think about how nice it would be if I didn't worry about that last bullet, but the thought gnaws at me like a squirrel with a pecan."

She blinked back the tears and sniffed. "Why do you stick a match into your mouth? You only seem to do it when you sense danger."

"If I tell you, you gotta promise not to tell a soul."

She gave a curt nod. "I promise."

"In the heat of a gunfight, my tongue rolls out of my

mouth. I damn near bit it off once. Biting down on a match keeps it in place where it belongs."

She laughed, a musical melody that he'd remember as long as he drew breath, and touched her fingers to the hair curling around his ears. "You are nothing like I expected."

"I could say the same about you." Her laughter dwindled along with her smile. He brought her hand to his lips, holding her gaze. "And that, lady, makes you so damned dangerous."

LILLIAN WATCHED WILDER walk through the fallow fields beyond the house. He'd insisted on taking his supper on the porch even though she invited him to join them inside. It wasn't reasonable to want to know everything about him. It wasn't wise to be glad that he was staying a little while longer. It wasn't logical to realize she might be falling in love with him.

Strolling through the tall grass and weeds, she saw him crouch down. When she reached him, he scooped up the dirt and sifted it through his fingers.

"It's good soil," he said. "What are you going to grow?"

She knelt beside him and shrugged. "I haven't a clue. I don't know anything about farming."

"Corn would be good."

Watching his gaze roam over the fields, she was left with the distinct impression that he could actually envision the corn growing. "Were you a farmer?"

He dumped the remaining dirt out of his palm, stood,

and slapped his hand against his thigh. "Once. A long time back."

She rose to her feet. "What turns a farmer into a hired gun?"

She watched his Adam's apple slowly rise and fall as he swallowed. "A desire to die."

In long strides, he strode across the fields. She hurried to catch up to him. "Why would you want to die?"

"Because I didn't want to live."

"Why?"

He staggered to a stop, and she nearly slammed into him.

"Why the sudden interest?" he asked.

"I've always been interested, but I think I was afraid to know the truth. What sort of man are you, Chance Wilder? A man offers you a fortune and you turn your back on it for a piece of string and a bent coin. You've killed twenty-four men, twenty-six counting Wade and that fella today."

"That's what they say."

She stared at him, comprehension slowly dawning. "*They say* you've killed twenty-six men. *They say* you're fast. *They say* you always work for the best offer. But you don't say." She angled her head thoughtfully. "How many have you killed?"

"Before I came to Lonesome?"

She nodded, wondering whether to welcome or dread the truth, if it was what she suspected or far worse than anything she could imagine.

"Eight."

Relief swamped her, washing away the tension that had mounted while she'd waited for his answer. He had killed, but not to the degree she'd believed. "Tell me about the woman in Dripping Springs. The one who paid you a pig."

"Two pigs. She paid me two pigs to make her neighbor think twice before trampling his herd through her garden."

"How did you stop him?"

"Paid him a visit, told her she was under my protection and that I'd take it kindly if he'd keep his cattle on his land. He obliged by putting up a fence."

She laughed lightly. "You're not as tough as you pretend to be."

He narrowed his eyes into silver slits. "I'm tough, lady. Never make the mistake of thinking I'm not. I've been on my own since I was fourteen."

"What happened when you were fourteen?"

He hesitated.

"Are you afraid to tell me?" she goaded. "Afraid I might realize you aren't so tough?"

She saw a muscle in his jaw clench.

"I went hunting . . . with my brother. James was four years older than I was. It's been ten years, but I can see him clearly—like he was standing in front of me. We lived in Palo Pinto. Lot of renegades and outlaws causing trouble back then." A far-off look came over his expression, as though his mind were traveling back to an earlier time, a different yet familiar place. "We separated, thinking we'd have better luck finding game. Then I heard him scream." Anguish reshaped the lines of his face. "By my count close to two dozen renegades had taken him by surprise. They were torturing him, and his screams for mercy were echoing around me. I couldn't save him."

Compassion swelled in her for the child who had witnessed his brother's anguish. It had nearly torn her heart in two to see Toby hurt when they'd been attacked in town. She couldn't fathom how Chance must have suffered hearing his brother's screams. "What did you do?"

As though catapulted from the past, he snapped his icy gaze to her. "I killed him. One bullet between the eyes. I've always been a damn good shot."

His words hit like a physical blow. The horror of what he'd done—not that he'd done it, but that he'd been left with no choice except to take his brother's life in order to spare him the torment. How much courage it must have taken. How much love. How much regret. Tears welling in her eyes, she touched his arm, knowing it was far too late for comfort but needing to offer it anyway. "I can't imagine how awful it must have been for you, but it was an act of mercy. I have no doubt that your brother was grateful to be spared further agony."

He laughed mirthlessly. "My parents didn't see it that way. They kicked me out with nothing but the clothes on my back. According to them, I should have at least tried to save him instead of taking the coward's way out."

They thought him a coward? Dear God, she thought he'd been more courageous than anyone had a right to be. He had to have known the demons that would haunt him after he pulled the trigger, yet he'd done it anyway.

He had to have known the doubts and regrets that would dog him.

"What you did was an incredibly selfless act of love. Had you attempted to rescue him, you would have suffered his fate, and in the end you would have both died."

He shrugged as though striving to shake off a fly. "Maybe. We'll never know. I only know that he's dead, and for a long time I wished I was, too." His voice had gone deeper, rougher, and while she knew he was striving to appear unaffected, he wasn't. "I went wild, got into fights, goaded men of disreputable character until they drew on me. But at the very last second, in spite of my best efforts not to give in, the desire to live always won out over the need to die."

Spinning on his heel, he strolled back to the house, a lone figure silhouetted by the retreating sun. Overcome with the sorrow of his tale, Lillian knelt in the dirt and wept for the boy he'd been, the boy who had been faced with a horrendous choice. And she wept for the man who still paid the price for the decision he'd made.

Chapter 7

LILLIAN LAY IN bed, unable to sleep. Shafts of moonlight pierced the room. When she closed her eyes, she saw Chance standing in the fields, reciting his tale in an emotionless voice. But his eyes, his silver eyes, had revealed his anguish.

She slipped out of bed. He wouldn't stay, and when he left, she feared he'd take a portion of her heart with him. She padded down the hallway and peeked into Toby's room. His face relaxed in innocent slumber, he was sprawled across his bed. His fingers were curled around the bent coin Chance had returned to him earlier in exchange for tending his horse. She closed his door quietly before walking out of the house.

The night was warm, the sky a blanket of stars. The full moon guided her journey to the barn. She climbed the ladder and peered into the loft. Chance stood beside the opening, gazing out, limned by moonlight. As she climbed higher, the ladder creaked.

"Go back to bed, lady," he said harshly, dismissing her without even bothering to look at her.

Taking an unsteady breath, she crawled forward, ignoring the straw pricking her through her nightgown, then stood and walked toward him. "Your parents were wrong to send you away."

"I'm a killer—"

"No, I don't think you are." She touched his arm, the place where she'd bandaged his wound earlier.

"I shouldn't have told you that story."

"Why? Because I might come to understand you, to care about you?"

"I hurt people, lady. That's what I do. And I hurt the worst those I care about the most."

Her heart soared with the unguarded admission that he felt something for her. "Hold me."

"Lady, I'm hanging on by a thin rope." Despair and something akin to fear delved into the depths of his silvery eyes. "If you don't get out of here, my gun's coming off and so are your clothes."

"I'm staying."

He slammed his eyes closed. "Please don't stay, Lillian," he pleaded, the words designed to make her leave, but his voice—rough and raw—communicated the opposite, a yearning so deep for her to remain that she couldn't have ignored it if she'd wanted.

"I'm not going anywhere," she said softly, "and there's

nothing you can say that will change my mind on this matter."

Opening his eyes, he cradled her cheek. "In a few days I'm leaving."

She nodded, her breath catching in her throat. "I know."

"No matter what happens tonight, I'll ride out of here and never look back."

Every doubt she had melted away with his words, with his continuing attempts to send her away, even though his desire for her was shimmering between them. Whatever else Chance Wilder might be, he was a man of honor. "I want to be here, tonight, with you."

She heard his breath hitch, and in the moonlight, she watched his Adam's apple slide up and down as he swallowed. So slowly, as though to give her time to change her mind, he reached down and untied the strip of leather that kept his gun anchored to his thigh. Even more slowly, he unbuckled his gun belt and set the gun and holster in the corner behind him. When once again he stood before her, she thought she saw a flicker of doubt flash within his eyes.

"What's gonna pass between us will make it harder for me to leave, but I will leave, Lillian," he whispered, cupping her face between his hands.

She smiled softly. "I like it when you say my name. You'll have a harder time forgetting me."

"I'll never forget you," he rasped. "Whenever I see a stormy sky, I'll remember the deep blue of your eyes." He pressed a kiss to each of her closed eyelids. "When the leaves turn in autumn, I'll remember the way your hair looked when the sun glistened over it." He rained kisses over her face and throat. "And when the night comes, I'll remember what it was like to hold you in my arms."

His words brought tears to her eyes. She knew she would forever remember him. His arms closed around her, pressing the soft curves of her body against the hardened planes of his. She had tended his wounds, but she longed to tend his heart. When his mouth covered hers, she denied him nothing. He groaned and she felt him shudder.

With nimble fingers, he unbuttoned her gown and slid it past her shoulders. The soft cotton traveled the length of her body and pooled quietly at her feet. She fought the urge to hide from his appreciative gaze. He never took his eyes from her as he stripped out of his own clothes. She stepped into his embrace, and he carried her down to the quilts spread out over the straw. Warm and protective, his body blanketed hers. She pressed a kiss to a scar on his chest. How she longed to ask him to seek another means of living, a means that would keep him out of harm's way. How would she bear it when the news came that the notorious gunslinger had been slain?

She fought back the depressing thoughts and wrapped her arms more tightly around him, as though by doing so, she could keep him with her forever. She slipped her hand behind his head, threading her fingers through his curling locks, and brought his mouth down to hers. Eagerly, she kissed him, desperate to send the reminders of death into the shadowed corners. "Say my name," she rasped.

"Lillian." Chance lifted his mouth from hers and held her gaze in the moonlight. If death weren't nipping at his heels, he'd offer her more than a roll in the hay. He'd give her all he had, little as it was.

But he'd been reminded today how easily something that touched him could touch her. He couldn't visit a town without keeping his gun holstered throughout his stay. Always someone would challenge him, always death followed in his footsteps.

He gave his hands the freedom to roam over every inch of her, memorizing the texture, the curves, the hollows. And where his hands traveled, his mouth followed, bringing her pleasure. Her soft moans were the sweetest sounds he'd ever heard. Her gentle touch ignited a fire that he feared might never burn out.

"Chance," she whispered with a ragged breath. He wanted to die hearing his name on her lips, feeling her hands on his flesh.

Rising above her, he joined his body to hers, felt her tightness close around him. He rocked against her, hearing her tiny cries grow with intensity as she met his thrusts. She held his gaze, and when her body arched beneath his, he thought he'd never seen anything more beautiful—and that beauty carried him to new heights.

Breathing heavily, he collapsed against her. He pressed a kiss to the hollow at the base of her throat where the moisture gathered like the dew on a petal. Then he rolled to his side, tucked her within the curve of his body, and drifted off to sleep.

LETHARGICALLY, LILLIAN AWAKENED. The warmth was gone, and in its place she felt an unaccountable cold. She glanced toward the loft opening. Chance stood there, the moonlight playing a shadow dance over his nudity. She thought he looked magnificent.

As though sensing her appreciative gaze, he turned. She was unprepared for the anger flashing in his silvery eyes.

"They say you were Jack Ward's whore," he said through gritted teeth.

She eased up onto her elbows. "That's what they say."

"They say he died in your bed."

She nodded. "He did."

"But you weren't his whore." He glanced down at his thigh, and she saw the thin shadowy trail that spotted his flesh, knew it was her blood. "Until tonight no man had ever bedded you." He faced her squarely. "I want to know exactly what Jack Ward was to you."

She swallowed hard. "He was my father."

CHANCE STARED AT Lillian as though she'd spoken words he'd never before heard. "Your father?"

She nodded jerkily, the moonlight shimmering off the tears welling within her huge eyes. He dropped to the quilt beside her and cradled her soft cheek within his roughened palm. Guilt gnawed at him. If he'd known she was untouched, he never would have laid a hand on her. "Why didn't you tell me?" he asked, his voice hoarse, his throat knotted with emotions that threatened to be his undoing. He didn't deserve someone as innocent as she was.

She lifted her bare shoulder slightly and snuggled her cheek more closely against his cupped palm. "Two reasons. I was afraid if I told you, that you wouldn't believe me, and I wasn't certain I could stand the pain of not being trusted to speak the truth." She turned her face and pressed a kiss against his hardened flesh. "But more, I was afraid if I told you the truth—if you knew I'd never lain with a man—you wouldn't touch me, and I wanted you to very badly."

He brushed a kiss across her temple, inhaling her sweet fragrance, mingling with the scent of the straw and their earlier lovemaking. "Ah, lady, you shouldn't have come to me. You deserve so much better."

"You would have sent me away if you'd known, wouldn't you?" she asked.

"Yes. Hell, I should have sent you away anyway." He leaned back and studied her. He wanted to tell her that she filled a hole inside of him that he hadn't even known existed. But telling her anything about his feelings might prompt her to reciprocate—and forgetting her was going to be damn near impossible as it was without any declaration of love. "Does John Ward know?"

She shook her head. "No. He was out of town when Toby and I arrived. I don't know why Jack didn't tell his family before he moved us here. He had plans to tell them about me as soon as John returned, but he never got the chance."

Chance leaned back on an elbow and trailed his fingers along the inside of her thigh. "Tell me everything."

She sighed heavily. "My mother met Jack Ward during the war. He served in Galveston. She fell in love with him, and I think . . ." Within her eyes, he saw the stark truth warring with what she wanted to accept as the truth. "I think he loved her. When she died, I went through her things and discovered a letter he'd written her shortly after the war ended. He was returning to his family, and he said he'd never forget her. I also found newspaper clippings she'd collected, all heralding his success as a rancher near Austin. The night he died, he brought me a letter she'd written to him after he left her in Galveston. She wished him a lifetime of happiness." Lillian clutched his arm. "But she didn't tell him about me."

"Then how did he find out?"

"I wrote him after Mother died. I thought he might want to know that she was gone."

"What about Toby's father?"

She smiled softly. "Shortly after I was born, Mother moved to Houston. She worked in a saloon. I think the bartender, Ben, must have loved Mother for years, but he felt he had nothing to offer her." She shrugged. "I'm not sure of the details, but I remember that she stopped looking tired all the time. He doted on her. They'd planned to marry, but he was killed in a barroom brawl. Afterward, Mother realized she was carrying Ben's child. We lived in a room over the saloon then. Wasn't fancy, but we had love. She died of influenza last year."

Chance was silent for several seconds, considering

what Lillian had told him. Then he asked, "So how did you come to be here?"

"After I wrote my letter to Jack Ward, to tell him Mother had died," she said, "he came to Houston and told me he intended to make things up to me. He had a little house and some land he deeded over to me. Toby and I always wanted a house. And I'd always longed for my own father's love, so we moved here. A few nights after we were settled in, Jack Ward brought me my mother's letter. He was reminiscing about her when suddenly he clutched his chest and collapsed. I got him to the bed, and he died in my arms. Everyone assumed I was his whore."

"And you didn't correct them?"

"Everyone was in a panic. Mrs. Ward was hysterical. John arrived the next day and wanted to protect her. I didn't think she'd appreciate knowing her husband had another child. I've thought of leaving, but this property is the only thing Jack Ward ever gave me, other than my life. I can't give it up."

"Then I'll do all in my power to see that you keep it." He shifted his body and laid her back down on the quilt. Covering her body with his, he kissed her tenderly. He understood her desire to hold onto the land, because in the short time he'd known her, she'd become important to him, made him wish that he was worth holding onto as well.

Chapter 8

THE LATE AFTERNOON air hung heavy around Chance as he walked among the trees lining the banks of the river, Lillian's small hand nestled within his larger one as though it belonged there. They'd brought the boy swimming, and Chance could hear the muted gurgling of the nearby flowing stream. They'd left the boy to give him some privacy as he put back on his clothes. Chance welcomed the excuse to be alone with Lillian. He was dying for an opportunity to kiss her.

He stopped walking and faced her. The sun had whispered across her face, leaving her cheeks glowing a rosy red. If he lived to be a hundred, he'd never forget the shape of her face. "I want to have a meeting with John Ward. I'm thinking the troubles would go away if he knew the truth."

She hesitated a moment before she nodded thoughtfully. "And when the troubles go away, you'll go away."

He saw the sorrow sweep into her eyes. He was both humbled and terrified with the knowledge that she cared for him. He lowered his head, touched his mouth to hers and kissed her, gathering the memories close so he could unfurl them at night beside the campfire. She welcomed him as no one else ever had. She made him want to stay—when he knew he had to go.

He drew back and brushed his thumb over her swollen lower lip. "I'm not what you need, lady."

"But you're what I want."

Explosions rent the still air. Chance felt the pain tear through his back as he pulled Lillian close, withdrew his gun, and plunged over the embankment, giving them some protection. They landed hard amid dry leaves and brush.

"Can you get to the boy and horses?" he asked.

"Who do you think is out there?"

"My guess is that Ward hired his gun. Ride out of here and get the sheriff. I'll hold them off while you get away."

He heard more gunfire, stretched up and got off two shots before quickly ducking back down. Several returning bullets chunked bits of bark off the nearby trees.

"You can't stay here," she told him.

"I've got no choice. Someone needs to distract him. Now go!"

She leaned forward as though to kiss him briefly, then reeled back, horror etched across her face as she stared at the bright red blood coating her hand. Wrenching his duster aside, she gasped at the blood flowing freely, drenching his shirt and trousers. His side felt as though someone had built a blazing fire within him.

"We've gotta get you to a doctor," she said.

He cradled her cheek, despising the way his hand trembled. He held her gaze, hating the truth he had to impart. "I'm hurt bad, Lillian. Take the boy and get to safety. Tell the sheriff that Ward finally did something he can arrest him for."

"I won't leave you to die. I'll send Toby—"

He grabbed her arm and jerked her close. "And who the hell is gonna take care of your brother if you're killed? You were a sweet roll in the hay, lady, but that's all you are to me. Now get the hell out of here."

She pulled back, tears brimming in her eyes. "That's a damn lie. You're just trying to make me leave."

He drew her against him, unable to stand the anguish in her eyes. He brushed his lips against her soft hair. "My life has meant nothing. For God's sake, let my death mean something. Take the time I can buy you and get out of here."

He heard her muffled sob before she withdrew from his hold and gave him a jerky nod. He slipped his shaking fingers into his pocket but couldn't latch onto a matchstick. She brushed his hand aside, reached into his pocket, withdrew a matchstick and slipped it into his mouth.

His voice nearly strangled him. "Thanks."

"I love you," she whispered hoarsely before scrambling down the embankment toward the horses and Toby. He peered over the edge and fired twice, taking satisfaction in a man's yell. Then he dropped back down. He looked over his shoulder and saw Lillian and Toby riding out. Relief swamped him along with the blackness. His final thought was that he'd finally acquired something worth living for, but it was too late.

SITTING UNEASILY ASTRIDE his horse on a rise, John Ward listened as the echo of guns firing rang from the trees. For his mother's sake, he wanted the woman run off. The fella he'd just hired would only get paid if he got the job done.

Riding along the river that separated his land from the whore's, keeping a look out for strays while he discussed with two of his men where he wanted a new barbed-wire fence strung up, he had instantly gone on alert when the first shots rang out. It sounded as though the man he'd hired was in the process of earning his money.

"Should we check it out, boss?" Guthrie asked.

John considered, then shook his head. "No."

"It's the gal's land," Hop said. "She might be in trouble."

"She's got Wilder looking out for her." Although, truth be told, it sounded like she had a whole army. Then he spotted her urging her horse into a gallop as she cleared a copse of trees and waved something white over her head. A flag of surrender. No, petticoats. He didn't want to recognize a spark of respect for her gumption.

She drew her horse to a halt. "John Ward, I'll give you everything you want if he doesn't die!"

He eased his horse forward. "Who?"

"Chance Wilder. Your man shot him. Stop him from killing him. Send someone for a doctor. Don't let him die."

"You're willing to give up the land and house for a gunslinger?"

She nodded quickly. "Please, help him."

Her plea, the worry in her eyes, almost had him feeling remorse for his actions and treatment of her. He hadn't gotten a good look at her the night he'd visited, but he could see her clearly now. She was so much younger than he'd thought. What had possessed his father to go after her? Had he wanted to recapture his youth, most of which he'd lost in the war?

Suddenly silence reigned.

Devastation washing over her pretty face, she jerked her head around to gaze back at the trees. He wouldn't feel guilty if the gunslinger was dead, but when she looked back at him, he knew he would have many a restless night if the man died.

"I swear I'll do whatever you want. But please—"

"Hop, head into town," he said, cutting her off before she could finish. "Fetch the doc and the land agent. Guthrie, check out what happened on the other side of the river. If Wilder is still alive, take him to—" He had to search for her name. He'd called her his father's whore ever since he'd discovered she existed. "—Miss Madison's."

"Yes, boss."

Both his men took off at a gallop. John could tell by the cloud of worry in her eyes that she wanted to return to Wilder, but she'd stayed to honor the bargain. He couldn't let her into his house, not where his mother might catch sight of her.

"How did you meet my father?" he asked.

"You don't get my history, Mr. Ward. All you get is my house."

He couldn't stop the small smile that formed. "My father always liked a woman with gumption." Not that his mother had fit that description. He'd always thought his parents an odd pairing, his mother constantly needing reassurance. But his father had pampered her, given her all she wanted, except a faithful husband.

John nodded in the direction of the trees. "Go on. I'll meet you at your place with the land agent. We'll finish this business today."

Without another word, she urged her horse into a gallop. A shame she brought such pain to his mother. He thought he might have enjoyed getting to know the gal.

THE RAIN FELL softly on his face, and the fragrance of roses in their first bloom wafted around him. He heard the voice of an angel whispering his name and felt her gentle fingers caress his brow. He'd expected to drop straight into Hell, and here he was: on the other side of Heaven.

Struggling through the agony, desperate to gaze upon the angel's face, he forced his eyes open. Darkness surrounded him and a halo of light circled the angel. Tears glistened over her lovely face as she smiled tenderly. His heart tightened with a bittersweet pain that made the throbbing in his side pale in comparison.

"Hello," she whispered, her voice low, as though she feared anything she might say would bring him pain.

He licked his parched lips. She brought a glass of water to his mouth. He drank slowly, having been shot too many times not to know better than to take his time adjusting to the land of the living. "I'm not dead," he croaked inanely.

Her smile widened. "No. You were lucky."

"The other fella?"

"You shot him a couple of times, but he's recovering as well, from what I understand."

"He'll be at my back someday."

"I don't think so. It's likely he lost the use of his arm, at least when it comes to drawing a gun."

"The boy?"

"Toby's fine."

"Good. Good." Nodding, he drifted back into oblivion.

Lillian pressed a kiss to Chance's brow before gently wiping her tears from his beloved face. They'd found him and the other man unconscious, lying in the dirt, bleeding into the ground. They'd brought Chance here and taken the hired gun to Ward's. Before she'd signed the deed over to John Ward, she'd made him promise to pay the man enough, offer him a position at his ranch, so he would never feel the need to seek revenge against Chance. She'd been surprised that Ward capitulated so quickly. He wasn't a bad man. She understood the reasons behind his actions. They were motivated by his love for his mother— just as hers were motivated by her love for Chance.

"Think he'll live?" Toby asked.

She glanced over her shoulder at her brother. "He'll be weak for a while, but his fever broke and the wound is healing, so I think he's going to recover."

"He ain't gonna like what you did, Lil."

She touched Toby's arm. "We're not going to tell him. It'll stay our secret."

His face skewed into unhappiness, Toby nodded.

Gently, she squeezed his shoulder. "And as hard as it'll be, we have to let him go."

Chapter 9

CHANCE SLUNG HIS saddlebags over his horse's rump. A week of being laid up in bed had nearly driven him insane. He hadn't regained all his strength, but he'd gained enough to know Lillian Madison was anxious to see his back headed down the road.

"Where will you go?" Toby asked.

"Whichever way the wind blows," he said. He darted a glance at the woman standing calmly on the porch, watching his actions as though they meant nothing to her, as though he meant nothing to her. "So how long do you think this 'understanding' with John Ward will last?" he asked.

"Forever. You were right. Once I explained everything, he was extremely accommodating. He won't bother me and Toby anymore."

He didn't believe her, not for one minute. Something had happened between the time he'd blacked out and the moment he'd awakened in her bed, but he wasn't exactly sure what. The woman had been incredibly vague with the details, refusing to meet his gaze whenever the topic came up. Even when she'd despised what he did for a living, she'd met his gaze head on. He was willing to bet his life that she was hiding something. With a great deal of effort, he pulled himself into the saddle.

"You got the string?" the boy asked.

Chance smiled. He was going to miss the kid. "Yep." He shifted his gaze to Lillian. His throat constricted and he knew he wouldn't be able to push out any words, so he simply touched his finger to the brim of his hat and gave a brusque nod. She could have been a statue standing there. She didn't even bother to lift a hand in farewell.

After guiding his horse past her, he began galloping toward the sunset. And he never once looked back.

"IT'S MY UNDERSTANDING that you won't be bothering Miss Madison anymore," Chance said, standing in John Ward's office.

"That's right."

"And how do I know you won't change your mind?"

"No reason for me to. She traded the deed to her land for your life."

Chance's gut knotted up so tightly, he nearly keeled over. "What?"

John Ward shook his head, smiling. "It was something to see. She came galloping up from the river, waving her petticoat like a white flag. Said you'd been shot. She swore she'd sign over the deed to her land if I sent one of my boys for the doctor. Couldn't pass up an offer like that. Brought the land agent along with the doctor, and she signed the deed over to me right on the spot. Now that you're well enough, she ought to be packing up and moving on."

"Where's she gonna go?"

"I've got no idea and I don't care. She'll be off the land and that's all that matters to me. Her presence was breaking my mother's heart."

"I imagine your father is rolling over in his grave," Chance said.

Ward stiffened. "He had no right to bring his whore here."

"She wasn't his whore. She's his daughter."

Chance heard a soft gasp. He spun around. A silver-haired woman stood in the doorway. She pounded her cane on the floor. "John, make this man take his bald-faced lies out of this house!"

John Ward studied his mother. "Are they lies, Mother? Or have you been dishonest with me?"

Tears filled her eyes, spilled over onto her papery cheeks. "I told him not to bring her here, but he said he owed her. He loved her mother during the war, but it was just to punish me because I wouldn't live in Galveston with him. I didn't want to be where the Yankees might be." She hit her cane on the floor. "I don't want her here."

"Why did you tell me she was father's whore?"

The elderly woman sank into a chair. "Because I knew you wouldn't send her away if you knew the truth. If you knew she is . . . your sister." She fairly spat out the last word. Chance wanted to feel sorry for her, but he couldn't, not when she'd caused Lillian so much pain.

Ward crossed the room and knelt before his mother. "You're punishing an innocent woman for the sins of my father."

"He had no right to parade her in front of me."

"He wasn't parading her," Ward said. "He was striving to make amends."

Chance strode across the room. Ward snapped his head around. "Where are you going?"

"I'm leaving. I found out what I came here to learn."

LILLIAN SAW THE rider silhouetted against the late afternoon sun. After setting the box into the back of the wagon, she lifted her hand to shield her eyes from the glare. Clothed in black, the man sat tall in the saddle. Her heart leapt into her throat. He wasn't supposed to return.

Toby rounded the corner. "Hey, Lil, can I—" He came to an abrupt halt. Then his eyes widened as the rider drew his horse to a halt. "Chance!" He bounded across the short expanse separating them. Smiling broadly, he craned his head so he could look up. "You came back!"

"Sure did," Chance said in a low voice as he slowly dismounted. Reaching into his pocket, he withdrew a length of frayed string. "Here, Toby, you can have this back."

Toby snatched it out of his hand. "Great! I was needing some string."

Lillian stared at Chance. "You said his name."

"Yes, I did, Lillian," he said as he stalked toward her, his eyes narrowed. "You gave Ward the deed to the land. You told me it was important to you."

"You're more important."

He jerked her into his embrace, and she felt the rapid pounding of his heart beneath her cheek. "Damn you, Lillian, why didn't you tell me?"

"Because I knew you'd get angry, or worse, you'd feel that you owed me, that you might decide you needed to look after me or see me situated somewhere else. I didn't want you beholden."

"Why did you give him the land?" he asked in a hoarse voice.

She tilted her head up and met his gaze. "Because I love you."

If she didn't know better, she would have thought he'd taken a good solid punch to the gut, but his silver eyes warmed. He cradled her face between his hands. "I've got some land west of here. There's nothing on it, except a couple of pigs—"

She shook her head. "Once before, I took land in place of a man's love. It's a poor substitute. I won't do it again."

"And what if my love comes with the land?" With his thumbs, he caressed her cheeks. "I don't know if it'll work, but I'm thinking if I hang up my gun and we live a quiet life for a while . . . maybe my reputation will fade. Right now all I have is a long stretch of lonesome waiting for me down the road, and I want more. I want a home, a wife, a family. I want you."

She smiled softly, her heart humming with happiness.

At the echo of thundering hooves, she turned her head. Chance released her and stepped back, slipping a match between his teeth. She didn't know if she could live like this, constantly wondering when the last bullet would come.

The rider drew his horse to a halt. Her heart slammed against her ribs as John Ward stared intensely down at her. Straightening her shoulders, angling her chin, she met his gaze.

"You have his eyes," he said quietly. "I didn't notice that before, and I should have."

Her knees weakened with the realization that he knew the truth—and how he'd come to know it. She looked at Chance. "You told him."

He nodded. "My temper got the best of me. Besides, he needed to know."

"I'm glad he told me," John said. "I owe you an apology, Miss . . . Ward. Your name should be Ward, and I'm ashamed my father didn't do right by you. Even more ashamed that I treated you unfairly, that I assumed the worst and reacted as though you deserved to be considered less. Why didn't you tell me?"

"You didn't give me much opportunity."

"But on the ridge, when you offered to trade back the house for Wilder's life—why not tell me then?"

"I didn't think it would make things between us any better. I doubted you'd believe me." She shook her head. "No, that's not it. We should be honest with each other now. The truth was, Mr. Ward, I wasn't certain I wanted to acknowledge being the sister of a man who was willing to do the things you were. Chance Wilder may be a gun-for-hire, but he's honest about it. Men who face him know what he is, know the odds. He never draws his gun first, he never goads. In spite of his occupation, I've never known him to be cruel. I wasn't certain the same applied to you."

Ward nodded. "Can't say I don't deserve that. I doubt it'll make you feel any kinder toward me knowing that I was striving to protect my mother, to spare her suffering. She told me you were my father's whore. I had no reason to doubt her." He glanced over at Toby. "Is he—"

"No, his father was someone else. Your father never saw my mother again after the war ended."

"So afterward he was loyal to my mother."

"That I can't say for sure, but knowing him for the short time I did, I believe he loved your mother and was faithful to her. War, I suspect, changes things for a time." She indicated the doorway behind her. "I'd invite you in for some coffee, but I've already packed up my cups."

He smiled, and in that smile, she saw her father. "I don't deserve your hospitality, but I hope at some point you'll make that offer again. But for now, if you'll come into town with me, I'll deed the land back over to you."

Chance slammed his eyes closed. Ward was giving her back the land. All his hopes and dreams died with the offer. This land given to her by her father was her dream, the symbol of his love, and Chance knew he couldn't stay, no matter how much he wished he could. He was too well known here, and too many people knew of his presence. Word would spread like wildfire.

"No, thank you, Mr. Ward," Lillian said softly. "I no longer want the property."

Chance opened his eyes. She was watching him. "I've been offered some land west of here, and I always take the best offer."

Chance felt his heart swell with love, and he knew he'd do all in his power to make certain she had accepted the best offer.

"At least let me pay you what the land is worth," Ward offered.

Lillian shook her head and smiled warmly at Chance. "I don't need the money, Mr. Ward. I already have what I want most."

Chance drew her into his arms, holding her close, knowing he'd never let her go, knowing that at long last the road ahead of him wasn't going to be lonely.

EPILOGUE

Five Years Later

PUSHING HERSELF UP from the rocking chair on the porch, Lillian Wilder pressed her hand against her swollen stomach where her unborn child kicked. She was hoping for a girl this time.

Walking to the edge of the porch, she saw her husband strolling in from the distant cornfields, his three-year-old son perched on his shoulders, Toby loping along beside them. She watched as Chance threw his head back and laughed, and she knew Toby had told him something outrageous. She loved Chance's laughter, loved his smiles, loved him.

She heard a rumble and glanced toward the road. Her breath caught at the sight of the unfamiliar wagon.

Slowly, she released her breath. Men looking to gain a reputation usually rode in on a horse. In the passing years only two had come to the farm seeking out the notorious Chance Wilder. They'd left disappointed, discovering that Chance Wilder could not be goaded, beaten, or threatened into strapping on his gun.

She didn't think the elderly couple pulling their wagon to a halt in front of her house had come to challenge Chance's fading reputation. She stepped off the porch. "Evening."

The man looked at her with a piercing silvery gaze. "We were told this is Chance Wilder's place."

She wiped her suddenly damp hands on her apron. "Yes, that's right. Chance is coming in from the fields now."

The man climbed down from the wagon, and then helped the woman to the ground. Her light blue gaze was riveted on Chance as he strode toward them. The older man slipped his arm around her shoulders and drew her close as though what needed to be faced was better faced together.

Chance's stride faltered and slowed as he neared the house. Wariness guarding his features, he came to stand beside Lillian, his eyes drawn to the couple. He wrapped his hands around his son and lifted him off his shoulders, setting him on the ground between him and Lillian. A heavy silence stretched between him and the couple. Lillian slipped her hand into Chance's, surprised to find his trembling.

Tears welled in the old woman's eyes and spilled

onto her cheeks. She pressed a shaking hand against her mouth. "Chance," she whispered brokenly.

"Mama," he croaked.

She held out her arms. "We're so sorry. Forgive us, son. Please forgive us."

Chance shook his head. "There's nothing to forgive, Mama."

Chance released Lillian's hand and crossed the short expanse, taking his mother into his arms, her heart-wrenching sobs echoing around them. "We were wrong, wrong to send you away," she lamented.

"It's all right," Chance murmured.

His father hesitated, then stepped forward to embrace his wife and son. They held each other for long moments as the years and regrets melted away. Finally Chance drew back. "I want you to meet my family."

He held his hand out to Lillian. She stepped within the circle of his arm. "This is Lillian, my wife."

Lillian smiled warmly. "I'm very happy to meet you. Chance has often spoken of you."

"This young fella is Toby, Lillian's brother," Chance said. "I consider him to be my brother, too."

Toby beamed up at him, and Chance ruffled his hair. Then he lifted his son into his arms. "And this is our son," he told his parents.

More tears welled in his mother's eyes. "Oh, Stephen, we have a grandchild. How wonderful! What's his name?"

Chance hesitated, shifting his gaze to Lillian. Nodding, she rubbed his shoulder.

"James," Chance said quietly. "We named him James."

In memory of the brother he'd lost, they had selected the name. Her chest tightening, Lillian watched as understanding dawned in the older couple's eyes. Chance had loved his brother, would never forget him, but he had finally reconciled his actions on that fateful day. They still haunted him, they always would. But rather than searching for a bullet, now Chance honored his brother's memory by tending the fields and his family. She didn't think his parents would ever truly understand what one shot from his rifle had cost him, but they were here now and it was long past time hearts began to heal.

"We were about to sit down to supper," Lillian said. "Will you join us?"

"We'd love to," Chance's mother said. "We have so many years to catch up on."

"Toby, why don't you show them where they can wash up?" Lillian suggested, sensing that Chance needed a moment.

With his wife standing beside him, Chance stayed back, watching his parents stroll to the house, James between them, holding their hands. Toby opened the door and led them inside.

Lillian slipped her arm around Chance, and he drew her more closely against his side.

"They hurt you, and yet you forgave them so easily," she said softly.

"If they hadn't sent me away, I wouldn't have you."

"I'm not worth the years of loneliness and pain—"

He touched his finger to her lips. "Lillian, you're worth so much more."

Lowering his mouth to hers, he kissed her deeply, tenderly. He remembered Toby's offer. He'd thought everything was a length of string, a harmonica, and a bent penny.

But everything had turned out to be love.

**Don't miss Lorraine Heath's next
spectacular historical romance!**

Keep reading for a sneak peek at

Once More, My Darling Rogue

Coming Summer 2014 from Avon Books

Once More, My Darling Rogue

AT THAT PRECISE moment Drake Darling wished to be
anywhere other than where he was, but he was well aware
that in life one did not always get what he wished for. On
occasion, he didn't even get what he deserved.

So he relied upon what he'd learned during his for-
mative years about deception and he pretended that he
was positively delighted, beside himself with joy, to be
the center of attention. He much preferred the shadows to
glittering ballrooms. He was most comfortable when not
noticed, but he was at best a chameleon. He knew how
to blend in even when the blending in took place within
a room with mirrored walls, gaslit chandeliers, and the
finest personages the aristocracy had to offer.

The one thing he was not feigning was his happiness
for Grace and Lovingdon. He considered Grace a sister,
even though their blood could not have been more opposite. For many years now he had been close to Lovingdon,

a confidant on occasion, but more often a hell-raiser of late. Until Grace had captured the duke's heart.

Therefore, Drake couldn't very well not attend the celebration of their marriage. Only minutes earlier he'd caught sight of the happy couple escaping the ballroom. Normally the bride and groom didn't attend the ball held in their honor, but Grace was far from conventional. She'd wanted to dance with her father one last time. The Duke of Greystone's eyesight was deteriorating, although only the family was aware of his affliction. Another reason Drake was here: to acknowledge his debt to the man and woman who had given him a home. His presence was expected, and so he gave no outward sign to the six young ladies surrounding him that he wished to be elsewhere. He always did whatever was required to ensure the duke and duchess had no regrets about taking him in.

They were so young, the ladies who smiled and batted their lashes at him. Even the ones who were on the far side of five and twenty were too innocent for his tastes. They were all light and airy as though burdens were unknown to them, as though life encompassed nothing more than enjoyment. He preferred his women with a bit more seasoning to them, savory, spicy, and tart.

"Boy."

An exception to his preference for the tart had arrived. The haughtiness of the voice set his teeth on edge. He should have known he'd not escape her notice for the entire evening. That Lady Ophelia Lyttleton was one of Grace's dearest friends was beyond his comprehension.

He didn't understand why the sister of his heart associated with such an arrogant miss when Grace was the sweetest, gentlest person he'd ever known. Stubborn to be sure, but she hadn't a mean bone in her body. Lady Ophelia could not claim the same. Her presence at his back proof enough.

The ladies who had been gifting him with their attention blinked repeatedly and went silent for the first time in more than two hours. Because they were there, because he was striving to give the appearance of being a gentleman, he would spare Lady Ophelia the embarrassment of ignoring her. Even though he suspected he would pay a price for his generosity. He always paid the price. The lady was quite adept at delivering stinging barbs.

Slowly he turned and arched a brow at the woman whose head failed to reach his shoulder. And yet in spite of her diminutive size, she managed to give the appearance of looking down on him. It was her long, pert, slender nose that tipped up ever so slightly on the end. She had been a constant aggravation whenever she visited with Grace and crossed paths with him. But devil's mistress that she was, she was very careful to slight him only when Grace wasn't about to witness her set-downs. Because he loved Grace too much to upset her—and she would be appalled to know he and her friend were not on particularly pleasant terms—he had borne Lady Ophelia's degradations, convinced that he was walking the high ground while she was slogging along in the muck.

It made no sense to him that such a beauty could be

such a resounding termagant. Her green eyes with the oval, exotic slant were challenging him with a sharpness that could slice into one's soul if he weren't careful. While he was twelve years her senior, as she had grown toward womanhood, she had mastered the art of making him feel as though he were a dog living in the quagmire of the gutters again. Not that others among the aristocracy hadn't made him feel the same from time to time, but still it irked more so when she was the one responsible for the cut to his pride.

"Boy," she repeated with a touch more arrogance, "do fetch me some champagne, and be quick about it."

As though he were a servant, as though he lived to serve her. Not that he found fault with those who served. Theirs was a more noble undertaking and their accomplishments far outstripped anything she might ever manage. She, who no doubt nibbled on chocolates in bed while reading a book, without thought regarding the effort that had gone behind placing both in her hand.

He considered telling her to fetch the champagne herself, but he knew she would view it as a victory, that she was hoping to get a rise out of him, wanted to prove that he wasn't gentleman enough not to insult a lady. Or perhaps she simply wanted to ensure that he knew his place. As though he could ever forget it. He bathed every night, scrubbed his body viciously, but he could not scrape the grime of the streets off his skin. His family had embraced him, their friends had embraced him, but he still knew what he was, knew from whence he'd come. If he told Lady Ophelia the truth about everything that lurked in his past, she would no doubt pale and the moonbeams that served for her hair would curl and shrivel in horror.

From the ladies circling about, he sensed their anticipation on the air, perhaps even the hope that he would put *her* in *her* place. He'd never understood the cattiness that he sometimes witnessed between women. He knew Grace had received her share of jealousy because her immense dowry had made men trip over themselves to gain her favor. But Lady O for all her dislike of him had remained loyal to Grace, had served as his sister's confidante, had been a true friend. She didn't deserve his disdain or a set-down in front of ladies who might have wished Grace less attention.

He tilted his head slightly. "As you desire, Lady Ophelia." He turned to the others. "I'll be but a moment, ladies, and then we can continue our discussion regarding the most alluring fragrances."

For some reason they had devised a little game that resulted in his striving to name the flower that scented their perfume. It required a lot of leaning in along with inhaling on his part, and soft sighs on theirs.

Lady Ophelia had arrived on a cloud of orchids that teased and taunted, promising forbidden pleasures that in spite of his best attempts to ignore, lured him. Of all the women, why the devil did she intrigue him? Perhaps because she offered such a challenge, had erected walls that only the most nimble could scale in order to gain the real treasure behind them. He was adept at reading people, but for the life of him he'd never been able to read her.

Twisting on his heel, he headed to the table where

champagne and sundry other refreshments were being poured. He was acutely aware of her gaze homed in on his back. He suspected if he looked over his shoulder, he would see her whispering with the other ladies, warning them off. Little did she realize that she would be doing him a favor if she could ensure that he was left in peace. He had committed to three more dances, and wouldn't disappoint his soon-to-be partners by heading to the gaming salon before he'd completed his obligations. Nor was he going to give Lady Ophelia the satisfaction of ruining his evening by sending him on errands. One glass was all she'd garner from him.

He didn't know why, two years ago at Grace's coming-out ball, he had asked Lady Ophelia to dance. He had thought she had grown into an exquisite creature, and she was Grace's friend. While she had often looked down her nose on him, she'd been a child then and he'd assumed she'd outgrown childish things. He couldn't have been more wrong. With a horrified look, she had given him a cut direct. Turned her back on him without even responding to his invitation. It had not spared his pride to realize that others had witnessed the rebuff.

Snatching up a flute of champagne from the table, he wended his way back through the throng, not at all surprised to find that she had moved on. He considered downing the bubbly brew but hard whiskey was more to his liking, and then he heard her seductive laughter. How the devil could an ice maiden have such a throaty, sensual laugh, a siren's song that arrowed straight to the groin?

Irritated with himself for being drawn to the sound,

he glanced back over his shoulder to spy her flirting outrageously with the Duke of Avendale and Viscount Langdon. Their families were well-respected, powerful, and wealthy. He was not surprised to see two other ladies in the group. The gents were sought-after, but just as he tended to avoid social affairs, so did they. Marriage was so far in their distant future that they wouldn't be able to see it with a spyglass. They were here only because they were close to both Grace and Lovingdon. But now that the happy couple had departed, he suspected Avendale and Langdon would be headed elsewhere for their entertainment.

Unlike Lady O they would invite him to join them.

Ophelia's laughter reached him again, only this time when the sound went silent, her gaze landed on him like a huge stone, then dipped to the champagne, and her lips tipped upward in triumph, just before she wrinkled her nose as though she smelled something quite unpleasant. Her face settling once more into deceptive loveliness, she shifted her gaze back to Avendale, summarily dismissing Drake in the process.

Unfortunately for her, he was no longer quite so easily dismissed.

OPHELIA KNEW A quick spurt of panic. Darling strode toward her with purpose in his step, his large hands—a workman's hands—dwarfing the flute he carried. His expression shouted that he was tossing down the gauntlet and she feared she might have misjudged his mood tonight, that managing him might be more challenging than she'd expected, but manage him she would. She would not be cowed, not by him, not by any other man for that matter.

He was a commoner who came from common beginnings. He might wear the outer trappings of a gentleman, but she had no doubt that deep down he was a scoundrel, with a scoundrel's ways, and a penchant toward sinful behavior.

She didn't know why that thought caused her to grow uncomfortably warm. It was the crowded room, the gaslit chandeliers, the layers of petticoats, and the tight corset. She certainly wasn't imagining those hands exploring her body. She was not of the streets. She was a lady. And ladies did not contemplate such things.

But as he neared, something within the black depths of his eyes twinkled as though he knew precisely where her errant thoughts had journeyed and was more than willing to serve as her companion on a sojourn into wickedness. He was not handsome, at least not classically so. His features were rugged, craggy, as though shaped by an angry god. His nose was too broad, his brow too wide. His jaw too square. She could see the beginning of shadow, bristles that hadn't the decency to wait until later to appear. Why was she wasting her time cataloguing each and every inch of him when she had lords aplenty willing to give her attention?

As he came to a halt in front of her, he gave his gaze free rein to take a leisurely stroll over her person. Breathing became difficult, and she had a horrid fear he would find her lacking. She drew back her shoulders. What did she care regarding his opinion of her, when his opinion was of no worth?

"Your champagne."

His rough, deep voice wove something dark and sensual around the words. She suspected he wasn't a silent lover, that he whispered naughty things into a woman's ear.

"You were so remarkably slow in retrieving it that I'm no longer of a mood to drink it."

"Surely you'll not deny yourself the pleasure of allowing these bubbles to tickle your palate."

He wrapped a wealth of meaning around the word *pleasure*. That he would be so bold as to speak to her with such disregard while others were near . . . it was not to be tolerated. But for the life of her, she could think of no witty rejoinder because he was studying her as though he could well imagine *her* tickling *his* palate.

"With your tarrying, I believe it has gone flat," she said, before turning her back on him. "Avendale, I believe you were discussing—"

Drake Darling had the audacity to wedge himself between her and the duke. His eyes were narrowed, his jaw taut. "Lady Ophelia, I must insist that you take the champagne."

"You, *boy*, are in no position to insist on anything where I am concerned."

His gloved finger tapped the side of the flute, while his gaze bored into hers, and she could fairly see the wheels of reprisal turning in his mind. She didn't know why she sought to provoke him, yet something about him unsettled her, always had. She wanted to put him in his place, to remind him—and herself—that he was beneath her. Her father had taken a belt to her backside and bare legs when he once caught her speaking with Darling. She'd been twelve at the time, but it wasn't a lesson easily forgotten. She was not to associate with anyone not of noble birth.

"So be it," he murmured, lifting the glass. He tilted back his head and downed the golden liquid in one long swallow. She could see only a bit of his muscles at his throat working, because a perfectly tied cravat hid the rest from view. But his neck, like the rest of him, was powerful. Moving aside the glass, he licked his lips, satisfaction glinting in his eyes. "Not at all flat. Quite pleasant, actually, like the kiss of a temptress."

Anger, hot and scalding, shot through her. He was mocking her, ridiculing her. It didn't matter that she had begun this little drama with her earlier request. He was supposed to scurry away when he realized she no longer had an interest in the champagne. He wasn't supposed to make her wonder if any lingered on his lips, if she might taste it there. "Boy—"

"It's been a good long while since I was a boy."

She angled her chin. "Boy, perhaps you would fetch us all some champagne."

"When hell freezes over, my lady."

He took a step toward her. She took a hasty step back. Triumph lit his eyes. Blast him. She would retreat no further.

A footman passed by, and without removing his gaze

from hers, Darling set the flute on the silver tray the servant carried. Then took another long step forward.

She fought to hold her ground, but she could inhale his intoxicating fragrance now. Earthy and rich, the scent of tobacco or perhaps sin. He eased closer—

Half a step back.

"Dance with me," he said.

"I beg your pardon?"

"You heard me."

She angled up her chin. "I don't dance with commoners."

"What are you afraid of?"

"I don't fear anything."

"Liar."

She darted her gaze to the left, the right. Without her noticing, he had managed to maneuver her into the shadows of an alcove and was now barring her way. Those she had been visiting with earlier were nowhere about. She should have known that Avendale and Langdon would side with this blackguard and escort her friends onto the dance floor, into the gardens, or off for refreshments. Blast them! Still, she'd not be intimidated by the likes of Drake Darling. "You, sir, are despicable."

"And you're a haughty miss who needs to be taught a lesson."

"I suppose you think you're the man to do it."

His eyes darkened, his gaze dropped to her lips, and she found herself taking three quick steps back. "Don't you dare," she whispered, hating that her voice sounded more like a plea than a demand.

"You've been poking the tiger for some years now. You can't always expect him to remain docile."

He had the right of it there. She didn't know why she had continually singled him out. Perhaps because she sensed a darkness in him, one that called to her, one that was dangerous to welcome.

"You're making a spectacle of us," she pointed out.

"We're in the shadows. No one is paying us any heed at all."

Like some great hulking predator, he advanced on her. While she knew it to be unwise, she retreated farther into the alcove until her back hit the wall. Her heart beat out an unsteady tattoo. Within her gloves, her palms grew damp. "If you do anything untoward, I'll scream."

He laughed darkly. "And risk being caught with a guttersnipe? I think not."

"You're a black-hearted scoundrel."

"Which is exactly why I intrigue you. You're bored with all the fancy gents hovering around you. They'd never think of touching you with ungloved hands."

She caught her breath as his warm, rough hand cradled the left side of her face. Such a massive hand, his fingers easing into her hair, the edge of his palm against her jaw, the pad of his thumb stroking her cheek.

"You're bored with gentlemen running about doing your bidding," he continued.

"I'm not bored." She hated how breathless she sounded, as though she'd been running up a never-ending hill. Her chest felt tight, painful.

"You're spoiled because everyone gives you what you

want. You've never had to work for anything. Not even a gentleman's attentions or affections."

"You know nothing at all about me." Her voice came out small, frightened. In her heart of hearts, she knew he wouldn't physically harm her, nor would he do anything to damage her reputation. Grace would never forgive him, and if she'd learned anything over the years, it was that he desperately wanted to please Grace and her family. But she feared he had the ability to glimpse into her shattered soul. Like called to like, dark to dark.

"I know more than you think, Lady Ophelia. Understand more than you can possibly imagine. You'll marry some proper lord, but I suspect you would very much like to waltz with the devil first."

"You're quite mistaken."

"Prove it."

Before she could respond, he settled his pliant mouth over hers. It was softer than she'd expected, hotter. His thumb grazed the corner of her mouth, over and over, as though it were part of the kiss. She felt his tongue outlining the seam between her lips, before tracing the outer edges. Once, twice, then returning to the center, but no longer content with the surface. With an insistence that should have frightened her, he urged her to part her lips. His tongue slid through, gliding over hers, velvet and silk. Inviting her to explore, to know the intimacies of his mouth as he was discovering hers.

She should have been repelled, horrified. Instead she was entranced, drawn into sensations such as she'd never experienced. He was so terribly talented at eliciting delicious responses that began at the tips of her toes and swirled ever upward, a tingling of nerve endings, a lethargic warmth, that weakened her knees, her resolve to push him away.

She heard a deep groan, felt a vibration against her fingers and realized she was clutching the lapels of his coat. Clinging to Drake Darling was all that was keeping her from melting into a puddle of pleasure at his feet. This was merely a kiss, an ancient dance of mouths, yet it was proving to be her undoing.

He drew back, triumph glittering in his eyes. "Five more minutes and I could have you divested of your clothing and on your ba—"

Crack!

Her gloved palm made contact with his cheek, startling him, startling herself as well, but she would not allow him to make her feel as though she were a whore. "You are not only disgusting but you overvalue your talents. I didn't enjoy your touch, your kiss, not in the least."

"Your moans implied otherwise."

She lifted her hand to deliver another blow, but he snagged her wrist, his long, thick fingers wrapping firmly around her slender bones. He could snap them so easily. She was breathing heavily, while he seemed to have no trouble at all finding air.

"One slap is all you get, my lady. I would have ceased my attentions with the slightest of protest from you. You can't now be angry because you wanted what I was offering."

"I want nothing at all to do with you. Now unhand me."

His fingers slowly unfurled. Snatching her hand free, she fisted it at her side. "You are no better than the muck I wipe off my shoes."

"Methinks the lady protests overmuch."

"May you rot in hell." She sidestepped around him, greatly relieved that he didn't attempt to stop her, slightly disappointed as well. Whatever was wrong with her? It was an odd thing to realize that with him she'd felt . . . safe. Completely, absolutely safe.

Which was ludicrous. He didn't like her. She didn't like him. He was simply striving to teach her a lesson. She could only hope that she'd taught him one: she wasn't a lady to be trifled with.

About the Author

LORRAINE HEATH always dreamed of being a writer.
After graduating from the University of Texas, she wrote
training manuals and computer code, but something was
always missing. After reading a romance novel, she not
only became hooked on the genre, but quickly realized
what her writing lacked: rebels, scoundrels, and rogues.
She's been writing about them ever since. Her work has
been recognized with numerous industry awards, including RWA's RITA® and a *Romantic Times* Career
Achievement Award. Her novels have appeared on the
USA Today and *New York Times* bestseller lists.

Visit www.AuthorTracker.com for exclusive information
on your favorite HarperCollins authors.